The Floridan Fraud
A Franc Merlot Mystery

Brian Viers is the author of six previous books. He is recognized for his contributions to business coaching and philanthropy. He and his wife, Sharon, spend their time between Illinois and Florida.

ALSO BY BRIAN L. VIERS

Silent Partner:
A True Story of Life, Death, Crime and Surrender

Insights from Our Silent Partner

Significant U:
7-Steps to Becoming Simply Significant

Holy Smokes:
Faith, Fellowship, and Fire

How to Sell Cars:
The Art of the Dealership

The Vintage Vendetta:
A Franc Merlot Mystery

The
Floridian Fraud

A Franc Merlot Mystery

by

Brian L. Viers

First Edition

ISBN: 979-8-9996384-0-3
Published by VIA Press Publishing
BrianViers.com

Book layout by Sharon Viers
Special thanks to Jeff Neben for historical reference
Printed in the United States of America

Disclaimer

This is a work of fiction. Any resemblance to actual persons, living or dead, events, or locales is entirely coincidental.

The Floridan Fraud

A Franc Merlot Mystery

Prologue

St. Petersburg, Florida — Present Day

Franc Merlot stepped off the curb and into the Florida sun, the warm breeze off Tampa Bay a stark contrast to the crisp mornings of Bordeaux, France. His jacket, loosely draped over one shoulder, clung to a man still caught between two worlds. One of wine and refinement, and another of shadows and questions.

The Vinoy loomed ahead, its Mediterranean Revival façade radiant in the early light. He took it in with narrow eyes, knowing he hadn't chosen the grand hotel for leisure. It was strategic. Intentional. Someone connected to the man who disappeared in Bordeaux had been spotted here. A whisper. A thread. Just enough for Franc to follow.

Several months had passed since the mystery began. Art handler, Gregory Caldwell, gone without a trace, and with him, the rumored disappearance of an unaccounted-for painting by famed French artist, Cézanne. Official channels claimed clerical errors. Land disputes. Misplaced documents. Then to discover Caldwell had simply "relocated." But Franc knew better. The way that man vanished... It wasn't accidental. It was orchestrated.

Franc had learned to trust hunches. They had saved his life before.

As he entered the cool lobby of the Vinoy, its polished marble and quiet opulence welcomed him like a page out of another century. He scanned the crowd spotting tourists, professionals, and many well-dressed guests, but none gave him a second glance.

That suited him.

He wasn't here to be seen.

He was here to find the truth, about the missing man, the painting no one dared to claim existed, and the powerful people who had kept it buried.

This time, he wouldn't walk away empty-handed.

Chapter One

Palms and Pretenses

The sun hung low over Tampa Bay, casting a warm glow across the terracotta roof and unmistakable pink exterior of the historic The Vinoy Resort and Golf Club. Franc Merlot stood outside the entrance beneath a pergola, trimmed in white, and lined with a canopy of palm trees, suitcase in one hand, sunglasses hiding the squint of transatlantic jet lag. The breeze off the water was different here, less earth and oak, more salt and mystery.

Florida, or the United States for that matter, wasn't his usual territory. He preferred cobblestones over boardwalks and vineyards over beach bars. Yet, here he was, stepping through the grand arched entry of The Vinoy, lured not by leisure, but by a hunch.

The American, a man once presumed missing in France, was here now, alive, well, and back to his old life as if none of it had happened. The same man whose so-called disappearance had set into motion a storm of deception across the south of France. And while the case had wrapped with satisfying ends, something still lingered. A gap in the timeline. A conversation unfinished.

Franc checked his bags with polite nods, noting the staff's crisp uniforms and the way they eyed him, eager to serve with polite curiosity. He wasn't a tourist. Not quite a guest. He was a man looking for what did not want to be found.

From the veranda, he could see across the street, the bay glinting in the distance and the marina where expensive boats bobbed in rhythm. He'd learn soon enough that paradise, like a vineyard, could grow secrets too. Especially when people were too busy looking at the sunset to notice what was cast in its shadow.

Franc removed his sunglasses as he entered the grand lobby, nodding to Jeffery, the concierge. "Tell me," he said casually, "does a man named Gregory Caldwell arrive often? Tall, well-dressed. Prefers whiskey over wine."

Jeffery, being the professional he is, hesitated, then merely smiled. Franc knew discretion was paramount here, but it was worth the try. And the hesitation was enough of a tell.

Franc smiled back, but the expression never reached his eyes.

"Thought so," he said jokingly, and walked toward the bar, the ghosts of Bordeaux trailing just behind him.

The Vinoy's hundred-year-old existence showcased such an elegant lobby, still steeped in coastal luxury. The centuries-old pecky cypress wooden beams on the ceiling, walls framing large arched windows, and the original porcelain tiles on the floors. Decorative painted wood trim, and the fresh scent of extravagant living presided over the salt air. Franc took a seat on a high back chair in the lounge, where the rhythm of classical jazz spilled softly from hidden speakers, the kind of music meant to relax you into forgetting what you came for.

A bartender with a clean white shirt, gray vest and the gait of someone who'd served the same elite faces for years approached. "What'll it be, sir?"

"Bordeaux. Left Bank, if you have it."

The bartender raised an eyebrow, impressed. "I think I can find something worthy of your taste."

Franc leaned back, scanning the guests. Two men in golf polo shirts and attire discussed the area's real estate boom. A couple seated nearby shared oysters. But no sign of Caldwell, yet.

A glass of wine arrived moments later. Franc took a slow sip, not to enjoy the flavor though it was excellent, but instead, buying some time. This was recon. The Vinoy was beautiful, no doubt. A perfect mask for truth. Behind the whitewashed walls and oceanfront smiles, he knew something more simmered.

That man hadn't disappeared without reason. Men with money and motive rarely moved without cause. And Franc had learned long ago: people don't vanish, they just shift their position.

He pulled out a slim aged leather notebook from his jacket. Inside, a name circled twice: Gregory Caldwell. Below it, underlined once, Vinoy Investment Partners, LLC. It was too polished. Too convenient. And the vineyard's name had appeared, faint but traceable, in a side document from Carly's earlier findings in Bordeaux. Holding company overlap.

He tapped his pen twice on the page.

Land, art, forgery. And now real estate?

Caldwell, the American, was no longer missing but that didn't mean he was safe. Or honest.

Franc pocketed the notebook and stood, nodding to the bartender. He would walk the grounds before nightfall. Somewhere between the docks, the club rooms, and the marina, someone knew more. And he was here to make sure they didn't stay quiet for long.

Chapter Two

Eyes on Aurora

Franc stepped onto Vinoy's manicured lawn, the evening air thick with humidity and the background repeating sounds of lapping waves against the nearby seawall. The marina stretched before him, a forest of masts swaying under the weight of wealth. Yachts gleamed in the twilight, their names - Second Chance, Elysian Dream - promising escape but whispering secrets. He adjusted his jacket, feeling the damp cling of Florida's heat, and scanned the docks for movement. Somewhere out there, Caldwell was playing a game, and Franc intended to learn the rules.

His notebook weighed heavy in his pocket, the circled name a tether to the recent past. Caldwell. The man who'd vanished from Bordeaux three months ago, leaving behind a trail of forged documents, land and vineyard disputes and a missing painting - a Cézanne, or so the rumors went. Carly's research had exposed the case back then, supposedly linking Caldwell to a French syndicate trading in stolen art and many other luxuries of the region. But the American had disappeared. Caldwell, his time in France and his motives, still a mystery to Franc and Carly.

Franc moved toward the marina, his polished shoes sinking slightly into the grass. The concierge's confirmation had been a start, Gregory Caldwell was a regular here, possibly a member, but regulars didn't hide in plain sight without a reason. Franc needed more than a name; he needed a thread to pull.

At the dock's edge, a young woman in a navy blazer stood beside a yacht, clipboard in hand. Her name tag read Sofia - Marina Staff. She was checking a roster, her brow furrowed as she scribbled notes. Franc approached, offering a disarming smile.

"Good evening," he said, his French accent softening the words. "A fine night for a sail, no?"

Sofia glanced up, startled, then returned his smile with a practiced one. "Not much sailing tonight, sir. Just routine checks. Can I help you?"

"Perhaps." Franc leaned casually against a bollard, his eyes flicking to the yacht behind her. Aurora's Promise. "I'm looking for a friend. Mr. Gregory Caldwell. I hear he's fond of the marina."

Her smile faltered, just for a moment, before she recovered. "Caldwell? I'm not sure I know him. We get a lot of guests here."

Franc nodded, letting the lie hang in the air. He'd seen that flicker in her eyes, recognition, followed by caution. "Of course. But a man like him, tall, silver hair, partial to rare whiskey, he stands out. Perhaps he's been on one of these boats? Aurora's Promise, maybe?"

Sofia's grip tightened on her clipboard. "I'd have to check the logs. Privacy, you understand."

"Naturally." Franc slipped a business card from his pocket, plain white with only his name and a France phone number. "If you recall anything, I'd be grateful. I'm staying here at The Vinoy. Room 316."

She took the card, her fingers brushing his, and nodded curtly. "I'll let you know."

As Franc turned to leave, he caught a glimpse of movement on the yacht's deck, a shadow, brief but deliberate, slipping below. Not a crew member. Someone who didn't want to be seen. His pulse quickened, but he kept his pace steady, strolling back toward the resort as if nothing had caught his eye.

Back in the Vinoy's lobby, Franc bypassed the lounge and headed for the elevators. He needed to cross-reference Carly's old files, still tucked in his suitcase. If Caldwell was tied to Aurora's Promise or Vinoy Investment Partners, there'd be a paper trail, however faint. Carly, his longtime friend and occasional investigative partner in Bordeaux, had a knack for digging up what others buried. Her last email, sent just before he boarded the plane, had hinted at a connection: Vinoy Investment Partners owns a stake in a local gallery. Check the art scene. Caldwell appears to have a taste for the finer things.

In his room, Franc spread the files across the desk. A list of shell companies, one linked to a vineyard, Château de Lirac. And now, Vinoy Investment Partners, LLC, with its vague ties to real estate and, if Carly was right, art. The pieces didn't fit yet, but they were starting to draw parallels.

He poured a glass of red wine, a favorite Bordeaux from a bottle he'd smuggled in his luggage. The American airports were lenient about such things. He sat by the window, watching the marina lights flicker. Caldwell hadn't vanished without reason. Men like him didn't retire; they reinvented. And St. Petersburg, with its galleries and waterfront wealth, was the perfect stage for a new act.

A knock at the door snapped him from his thoughts. He set the glass down, hand drifting to the small Beretta he kept in his suitcase. Old habits.

"Who is it?" he called, voice calm but firm.

"Room service," came the reply, a woman's voice, clipped and professional.

Franc hadn't ordered anything. He crossed to the door, peered through the peephole, and saw a uniformed staff member, a woman, mid-30s, with dark hair pulled back and a tray in her hands. No visible threat, but his instincts prickled. He opened the door, keeping his body angled.

"I didn't order room service," he said, studying her.

She smiled, unfazed. "Compliments of the house, Mr. Merlot. A welcome gift for our international guests." She lifted the tray's cover, revealing a bottle of whiskey, single malt, expensive and a note.

Franc took the tray; his eyes locked on hers. "Who sent this?"

"The management," she said smoothly. "Enjoy your stay."

She was gone before he could press further. He set the tray on the desk and unfolded the note.

In neat, handwritten script: *Welcome to St. Petersburg, Detective. Some shadows are best left alone.*

Franc's jaw tightened. He glanced at the whiskey, then back at the marina, where Aurora's Promise bobbed silently in the dark.

Caldwell, or someone close to him knew he was here. And they weren't wasting time.

Chapter Three

Tides of Truth

Franc stood at the edge of the Vinoy's marina, the morning sun glinting off the water like shards of a shattered mirror. The note from last night weighing on his mind: Some shadows are best left alone. A warning, yes, but also a challenge. Whoever was pulling the strings knew Franc was here, and they were already playing defense. His hunch corroborated, perhaps.

He'd barely slept, his room at the Vinoy feeling less like a sanctuary and more like a stage. The whiskey bottle remained untouched on the desk, its amber glow taunting him. He didn't trust gifts, especially not ones delivered with cryptic notes. Instead, he'd spent the night poring over Carly's files, her meticulous notes, a lifeline to the past. Bordeaux, Nice, Monaco. Caldwell, having appeared briefly, then disappeared leaving only questions and a faint trail of forged signatures. Now, in St. Petersburg, the scent established again, and the trail was warming. How could a simple land dispute over generational vineyard ownership in France involve the American, Gregory Caldwell and his ties to the LLC?

Carly, back in Bordeaux, had traced Caldwell's movements to a shady auction house, her fingers flying over her laptop as she uncovered shell companies tied to Château de Lirac. They'd shared many dinners and conversations over this case. Now she was oceans apart.

He shook off the memory and focused on the marina. Aurora's Promise securely tied to the dock's end slip, its deck empty in the morning light. The shadow he'd glimpsed last night hadn't reappeared, but Sofia, the marina staffer, had known more than she'd let on. Franc needed leverage, and he needed it fast.

His phone buzzed in his pocket.

A text from Carly:

> *Found something. Vinoy Investment Partners linked to a gallery on Central Ave - Sunlit Canvas. Caldwell's name popped up in a donor list. Be careful, Franc. He's not alone.*

Franc's lips twitched into a half-smile. Amazed. Carly, always one step ahead. She was an expert on new technology and advanced internet scraping software. He typed a quick reply, Merci, mon amie. Keep digging. Then pocketed the phone, pondering Sunlit Canvas. A gallery was the perfect front for Caldwell's old tricks: art, money, and secrets, all wrapped in a veneer of respectability.

Still early in the morning, he made his way along the waterfront, the Vinoy's pastel elegance giving way to the vibrant pulse of downtown St. Petersburg.

Central Avenue was also starting to wake up from the previous night's excitement. Two blocks up, Franc slipped into what appeared to be a staple of an old establishment called Central Cigar. He searched the vast inventory, an encased glass wall humidor until he found his preferred stick, then paired it with another staple, a shot of their signature fresh ground espresso. He meandered outside and found a comfortable chair to buy time. The street flourished with an occasional street hustler panhandling, artists sketching local scenes, and delivery drivers replenishing the establishment's alcohol inventory depleted from the prior night. People watching would pass the time until Sunlit Canvas soon opened its doors at noon.

The building was a sleek, modern space wedged between a café and a boutique, its glass exterior reflecting the street like a polished lie. A sign in the window advertised an upcoming exhibit: Tides of Expression, New Works by Local Visionaries.

Franc pushed through the door, a bell chiming softly. The gallery was cool and quiet, white walls with tall ceilings showcasing vivid abstracts and coastal landscapes. A woman in her mid-40s stood near a painting of a stormy sea, her auburn hair pulled into a loose bun, linen blue dress as crisp as the morning. She turned, her eyes sharp but welcoming.

"Bonjour," Franc said, letting his accent linger. "A beautiful space. I'm looking for something… unique."

She smiled, stepping forward. "You've come to the right place, Mr.…?"

"Merlot. Franc Merlot." He extended his hand, noting the faint callus on her palm as they shook. An artist, perhaps, as well as a curator. "I'm interested in your donors. A friend of mine, Mr. Gregory Caldwell, speaks highly of this gallery."

Her smile didn't waver, but her posture stiffened, a subtle shift Franc caught like a scent on the breeze. "Caldwell? A generous supporter, yes. I'm Elena Voss, the gallery director. May I ask what brings you here? Are you a collector?"

"A connoisseur, let's say." Franc wandered toward a painting, a swirl of blues and greens that screamed money but lacked soul. "I'm visiting from France. Gregory and I have... unfinished business. I was hoping to find him here."

Elena's eyes flicked to the door, then back to Franc. "I'm afraid Mr. Caldwell doesn't frequent the gallery himself. He's more of a silent partner. But I can pass along a message."

"That won't be necessary." Franc's tone was light, but his gaze held hers. "I'll find him myself. Though I'm curious, the Vinoy Investment Partners. They're involved here, yes? Quite a portfolio for a real estate firm."

Elena's smile tightened. "They're investors in local culture, as are most of the developers working here in Pinellas County. Art, real estate, it's all about building community."

"Of course," Franc said, stepping closer to a sculpture of twisted metal. "And yet, I find the community often hides its true face. Like a forged signature."

Caught off guard, her laugh was sharp, a little too loud. Forced. "You have a poet's tongue, Mr. Merlot. But I assure you, our art is authentic."

Franc nodded, letting the silence stretch. He'd struck a nerve, though he wasn't sure which one. Elena Voss was no mere curator, she was guarding something, or someone. He handed her his card, the same plain one he'd given Sofia. "If Mr. Caldwell surfaces, tell him I'm staying at The Vinoy. He'll know why."

As he left the gallery, the bell chimed behind him. Franc felt the weight of eyes on his back. Not only Elena's, but someone else's, watching from a distance down Central Avenue. He kept his pace steady, his senses sharp. Caldwell too, was close, he could feel it but the man was a ghost, slipping through cracks Franc hadn't yet found.

Back at the Vinoy, he found another surprise waiting in his room. The whiskey bottle was gone, replaced by a single white orchid, its petals stark against the desk. No note this time, but the message was clear: someone was toying with him, and they were not afraid to show their access.

Franc picked up the orchid, its scent faint but nostalgic. He thought of Carly, her warning echoing in his mind: He's not alone. Caldwell had allies, and they were circling. But Franc Merlot had never been one to back down from a chase, no matter how high the barrier stood in his way.

Chapter Four

Bourbon and Bargains

The Vinoy's private club lounge was a sanctuary of lowlights and white leather, where the clink of ice in bourbon glasses mingled with the murmur of deals being struck. Franc Merlot sat at a corner table, his glass of Bordeaux a deliberate contrast to the amber drinks around him. The room smelled of wealth, polished wood, and the faint tang of ambition. He'd chosen this spot to meet Mike Delaney, a name from a past case that now felt like a lifeline in St. Petersburg's labyrinth of secrets.

Meeting Mike had been a chance encounter years ago, during a brief trip to Florida for a smuggling case. A younger Franc, still green behind the ears, had crossed paths with the prominent attorney at a Tampa courthouse, where Mike's quick wit and easy charm had defused a tense negotiation. They had shared a drink afterward, Mike's bourbon to Franc's wine, and parted with a promise to reconnect. Now, with Gregory Caldwell's shadow looming, Franc needed Mike's knack for knowing the city's pulse.

The door swung open, and there he was, Mike Delaney, striding in with the confidence of a man who owned the room, or at least knew its secrets. His navy suit was tailored but relaxed, his tie loosened just enough to signal he wasn't here to impress. His hair, now streaked with silver, caught the light, and his smile was as warm as Franc remembered.

"Franc Merlot, as I live and breathe," Mike drawled, extending a hand. "You look like you haven't aged a day, though that coat's gotta be murder in this heat."

Franc rose, shaking Mike's hand, returning a smile. "Some habits die hard, Mike. Good to see you haven't lost your charm."

"Practice makes perfect." Mike slid into the chair opposite, signaling the bartender with a lazy wave. "Bourbon, neat. And another of whatever my French friend's drinking." He leaned back, studying Franc. "So, what brings you back to our little paradise? Not the beaches, I'm guessing."

Franc sipped his wine, weighing how much to reveal. Mike's affability was disarming, but Franc had learned to trust his instincts over smiles. "A man named Caldwell, Gregory Caldwell" he said, watching Mike's face. "You might know him. Tall, silver hair, connoisseur of fine whiskey. Seems to have a fondness for the Vinoy and downtown St. Pete."

Mike's expression didn't flicker, but his fingers paused on the table, a tell Franc filed away. "Gregory Caldwell, huh? Rings a bell. Big player in some of the local ventures. Real estate, mostly. Why's he on your radar?"

"He vanished in Bordeaux three months ago," Franc said, his voice low. "Left a trail of forged documents and possibly a missing Cézanne. My partner, Carly, and I chased his ghost, false leads that is, through Nice and Monaco, only to find the mysterious American wasn't harmed, instead he'd resurfaced here, living like he never left. I'm here to find out why."

Mike's bourbon arrived, and he took a slow sip, his eyes never leaving Franc. "Sounds like a hell of a story. But people come to St. Petersburg to start over, Franc. Not everyone's hiding something."

"Everyone's hiding something," Franc countered, leaning forward. "Caldwell's tied to Vinoy Investment Partners, which owns a stake in Sunlit Canvas, a gallery on Central Avenue. I met the director, Elena Voss, today. She's protective of him. Too protective."

Mike chuckled, but there was an edge to it. "You don't waste time, do you? Vinoy Investment Partners are big players around here. They fund half the waterfront projects, from condos to marinas. Sunlit Canvas is one of their pet projects. Art's an indiscriminate way to move money, if you catch my drift."

Franc's pulse quickened. Mike's tone was casual, but he was dropping breadcrumbs. "Money, or something else? Caldwell's not new to forgery. I'm wondering if he's painting a new picture here, literally, or otherwise."

Mike swirled his bourbon, his gaze drifting to the lounge's window, where the pier lights flickered. "You're wading in deep water, my friend. He's got friends in high places. Many developers, council members, even a few judges. My firm managed some of their contracts. Nothing shady on paper, but…" He trailed off, his smile fading.

"But?" Franc pressed, his voice sharp.

Mike leaned in, lowering his voice. "Let's just say some deals move faster than they should. Property transfers, zoning changes. Vinoy Investment Partners has a way of making things happen. And Gregory Caldwell? He's not the type to sit quietly on the sidelines."

Franc nodded, his mind racing. Mike's information confirmed Carly's suspicions: Caldwell was entrenched in St. Petersburg's power structure, and the gallery was likely another front. But for what? Art forgery, money laundering, or something bigger? And why the warnings, the whiskey, the orchid?

"Mike," Franc said, setting his glass down. "You know this city. If I wanted to get close to Caldwell, where would I start? The marina? The gallery? Or somewhere else?"

Mike hesitated, his fingers tapping the table. "There's a charity event here tomorrow night. Black-tie, big money. Caldwell's bound to show, his type never misses a chance to rub elbows. I can get you on the guest list, but you'll owe me one."

Franc smiled, genuine this time. "I always pay my debts."

As Mike stood to leave, he clapped Franc on the shoulder. "Watch your back, Franc. This town's all sunshine on the surface, but the people of the world stay the same."

Franc watched him go, the lounge's south music filling the silence. Mike was an ally, but that quiet tension, the pause, the guarded words lingered. Did he know more than he was letting on? Or was he just another player in St. Petersburg's upper echelon?

Back in his room, Franc found the orchid still on his desk, its petals curling slightly in the air-conditioned chill. He opened his laptop and fired off an email to Carly:

> *Gregory Caldwell's tied to Vinoy Investment Partners and Sunlit Canvas. Met a local attorney, Mike Delaney who I suspect knows more than he says. A charity event tomorrow may bring answers. Any updates on Château de Lirac?*

He hit send, then leaned back, staring at the marina, backlit by the beautiful new pier. Since Franc's last visit the old pier had been torn down with only talks of one day designing and building another.

Tomorrow, he'd step into Caldwell's world. But tonight, he'd prepare for the shadows and the man who cast them.

Chapter Five

Masks and Motives

The Vinoy's grand ballroom shimmered under crystal chandeliers, a sea of black ties and sequined gowns swirling to the soft hum of a string quartet. Franc Merlot stood near a marble pillar, his tailored suit blending seamlessly with the crowd, though his eyes betrayed him, sharp, restless, scanning every face. The charity event was a masquerade of wealth, St. Petersburg and beyond, the elite patrons raising glasses to art and progress while trading secrets in hushed tones. Caldwell, Mike had promised he would be here. And Franc was ready to pull the thread that would unravel the man's carefully woven return.

Just three months ago, in Bordeaux, the account of a missing American first made headlines. No photo, no details, just a whisper of a man who'd asked too many questions about Château de Lirac's vintage before vanishing. Franc and Carly had dug, chasing leads through auction houses and vineyard records, but the trail ended in silence. No body, no ransom, no proof, just rumors of foul play and a Cézanne painting that never resurfaced. They'd assumed him dead, another ghost in a case that refused to close. Until now.

Franc sipped his vintage red, a small anchor in this foreign tide.

Carly's latest email burned in his mind:

> *Château de Lirac's parent company has ties to Vinoy Investment Partners. Shell within a shell. Caldwell donated to Sunlit Canvas last month. Check the guest list.*

The words were clinical, but Franc could hear her voice, that faint lilt that always steadied him. He hadn't replied yet, hadn't found the words to bridge the distance between Bordeaux and this humid, glittering night.

"Enjoying the view?" Mike Delaney's drawl cut through his thoughts. The attorney appeared at his side, a bourbon in hand, his smile as polished as the ballroom floor. "Told you this was the place to be. Half the city council's here, plus a few folks who'd rather stay off the guest list."

Franc tilted his head, catching Mike's gaze. "Including Caldwell?"

Mike's smile didn't falter, but his eyes flicked to the crowd. "Patience, my friend. He's not one for early arrivals. Try the bar. His whiskey habit's a dead giveaway."

Franc followed Mike's gesture to the far end of the ballroom, where a mahogany bar gleamed under soft lights. A tall man stood there, silver hair catching the glow, his posture too deliberate to be casual. Franc's pulse quickened. Caldwell? No, too young. But the man's glance toward the ballroom's entrance was furtive, practiced, like someone expecting to make an appearance known.

"Mike," Franc said, keeping his voice low, "you've been straight with me so far. But I need to know: is he one of your clients?"

Mike's laugh was easy, but his fingers tightened around his glass. "You don't pull punches, do you? No, he's not mine. But my firm has handled work for Vinoy Investment Partners, I told you. Caldwell's name comes up in those circles. Let's just say he's skilled at making friends and enemies."

Franc nodded, filing away the deflection. Mike was a connector, as he'd remembered, but connectors often played both sides. "Enemies like the ones who leave orchids in hotel rooms?"

Mike's brow lifted, just a fraction. "Orchids? You've got my attention."

Before Franc could elaborate, a ripple moved through the crowd. Elena Voss, the Sunlit Canvas director, glided into view, her auburn hair striking against a deep emerald gown. She was speaking to a man in a charcoal suit, his back to Franc, but the way Elena's hand lingered on his arm screamed familiarity. And one noticeable difference, her left hand now showcased a massive luster of diamonds. A detail impossible for Franc to have missed at the gallery. Franc's instincts flared. He excused himself from Mike and edged closer, weaving through guests with the grace of a man who'd navigated far darker rooms.

Elena's voice carried as he approached, low but clear. "- need to be careful, darling. Not everyone here is as charmed as they seem."

The man turned slightly, and Franc froze. Tall, silver hair, a whiskey glass in hand. Caldwell. The face matched the grainy photo Carly had dug up, older now but unmistakable. His eyes, sharp and calculating, swept the room before settling briefly on Franc. A flicker of recognition passed between them before Caldwell turned back to Elena.

Franc's hand slipped to his pocket, brushing the leather notebook where Gregory Caldwell's name sat circled. He wanted to confront him, to demand answers about Bordeaux, the disappearance and link to the Cézanne. But not here, not yet. The ballroom was a chessboard, and Caldwell was no pawn.

As Franc stepped back, a hand grazed his elbow. He turned to find Sofia, the marina staffer, dressed not in her navy blazer but in a sleek black dress, her clipboard replaced by a champagne flute. Her eyes were wide, urgent, and she leaned close, her voice barely a whisper.

"Mr. Merlot, you need to leave. Now."

Franc's jaw tightened. "Why the rush, Sofia? Something on Aurora's Promise I should know about?"

Her gaze darted to Caldwell, then back to Franc. "You're asking questions that get people hurt. That orchid wasn't a gift. It was a warning. Meet me at the marina, midnight. I'll tell you what I can."

Before Franc could respond, Sofia melted into the crowd, her black dress a shadow among the glitter. He glanced back at Caldwell, but the man was gone, Elena now alone at the bar, her smile fixed as she chatted with a guest. Franc's mind raced. Sofia's fear was real, but was she an ally or a lure? And Caldwell, had he seen Franc, or was that glance a coincidence?

Mike rejoined him, his expression unreadable. "Find what you were looking for?"

"Not yet," Franc said, his eyes on the spot where Caldwell had stood. "But I'm getting closer."

As the quartet struck up a new waltz, Franc felt the weight of the night settle on his shoulders. Gregory Caldwell was here, alive, and untouchable. But Sofia's warning, the orchid, and Mike's guarded answers told Franc one thing: the shadows of Bordeaux had followed him to St. Petersburg, and they were closing in.

Chapter Six

Whispers on the Water

The marina at midnight was a different beast, its daytime sparkle replaced by a stillness that clung like damp silk. The yachts loomed like silent sentinels, their hulls creaking softly against the docks. Franc Merlot stood in the shadow of a palm tree; his trench coat swapped for a dark blazer to blend with the night. The air was thick, and Sofia's warning echoed in his mind: You're asking questions that get people hurt. He'd come to the Vinoy to find

Caldwell, but the man's shadow was proving longer, and darker than he'd expected.

Bordeaux felt a lifetime away, yet it haunted him. Caldwell's disappearance had been a puzzle with too many pieces: a newspaper clipping about a missing American, whispers of his questions about old vineyard families, and rumors of a Cézanne stolen from a private collector in Nice. Franc and Carly had chased those shadows through Bordeaux's cobblestone streets, sifting through auction records and vineyard ledgers, only to find dead ends. Caldwell's inquiries were too pointed, too curious, having suggested ties to the underworld, a world of art heists and Monaco's gilded criminals. They'd thought him dead, a victim of his own ambition. But instead, he'd quietly slipped away, back to Florida.

Now, standing by Aurora's Promise, Franc felt the weight of that failure. Her email from earlier still burned in his pocket: …*Watch yourself.* Her words were a lifeline, but they carried a warmth he couldn't shake, a memory of her hand brushing his as they pored over files in a Bordeaux café. He pushed the thought aside. Focus. Gregory Caldwell was here, alive, and Franc was done with wild goose chases.

A soft shuffle broke the silence. Sofia emerged from the dock's edge, her black dress from the charity event replaced by jeans and a hoodie, her eyes darting like a cornered animal. She clutched a small envelope, her knuckles white broke through the darkness.

"Mr. Merlot," she whispered, glancing over her shoulder. "I shouldn't be here. If they find out..."

"Who's 'they'?" Franc stepped closer, his voice low but firm. "Caldwell? Vinoy Investment Partners? Or someone else?"

Sofia hesitated, her breath catching. "I don't know names. Just... people who watch. They know you're asking about him. About the yacht." She thrust the envelope into his hands. "This was in Aurora's logbook. I wasn't supposed to see it."

Franc opened the envelope, pulling out a folded sheet, a shipping manifest, dated two weeks ago. It listed a crate from Bordeaux, marked Château de

Lirac, Private Reserve, destined for Sunlit Canvas via Vinoy Investment Partners. The signature at the bottom was illegible, but the destination caught his eye: Central Avenue, St. Petersburg. Not wine, he thought. Not with Caldwell's history. He tucked the manifest into his blazer, his mind racing. Art? Forged documents? Or something heavier?

"Why help me, Sofia?" he asked, studying her. "You're scared. What's in it for you?"

Her eyes flicked to the yacht, then back to him. "I don't want trouble. But Gregory Caldwell… he's not what he seems. He was on Aurora's Promise last week, meeting someone. They talked about 'delivery' and 'keeping it quiet.' I heard your name."

Franc's blood ran cold. "My name?"

Before Sofia could answer, a beam of light cut across the dock, a flashlight, sweeping from the marina's entrance. Sofia gasped, grabbing Franc's arm. "Go. Now. Someone's coming."

Franc didn't argue. He pulled her into the shadow of a nearby yacht, crouching as footsteps approached.

The steps heavy, deliberate, not the casual stroll of a security guard. The flashlight beam danced closer, and a man's voice growled, "Check the docks."

Sofia's hand trembled in Franc's grip, but he held steady, his mind sharp. He whispered, "Stay low. We'll move when they pass."

The footsteps paused, then shifted toward Aurora's Promise. Franc glimpsed two figures, broad-shouldered, one holding the flashlight, the other a phone pressed to his ear. "No sign yet," the man on the phone muttered.

Franc's jaw tightened. Maybe now they were after Sofia…and him. He weighed his options: confront them, risking a fight he couldn't win, or slip away and live to ask more questions. He chose the latter, guiding Sofia along the dock's edge, their steps muffled by the lapping water. They reached a small utility shed, ducking inside just as the flashlight swept past.

Sofia's voice was barely audible. "I'm sorry. I didn't know they'd follow me."

"Who are they?" Franc pressed, his eyes locked on hers.

"I don't know," she insisted. "Caldwell's people. They watch the marina, the gallery. They know you're digging."

Franc nodded, his mind piecing it together. Caldwell's questions in Bordeaux about vineyard families, their wealth, and their secrets hadn't been random. He'd been probing, perhaps for leverage in an art heist or a deal gone wrong. His "disappearance" was an escape, and now, in St. Petersburg, he was rebuilding, using Vinoy Investment Partners and Sunlit Canvas as fronts. But for what? And why was Franc's name on their lips?

"Go now and be careful," he told Sofia. "Lock your door, don't open it for anyone. I'll find you tomorrow."

She nodded, slipping away into the dark. Franc waited, listening as the footsteps faded, then made his way back to the resort, the manifest burning a hole in his pocket. In his room, he found the orchid still on the desk, its petals now wilting.

He opened his laptop and typed a quick email to Carly:

> *Found a manifest - Château de Lirac to Sunlit Canvas, via Vinoy Investment Partners. Caldwell's people are watching me. Any trace of that Cézanne or Bordeaux families he targeted?*

He hit send, then poured a glass of Bordeaux, staring out at the marina momentarily below, before pulling his curtains closed. Caldwell had played them all in France, slipping away while Franc and Carly chased shadows. Now, in St. Petersburg, it was game on again. But this time, Franc was in his world, and he wasn't leaving without answers.

Chapter Seven

Echoes in the Hall

Morning light filtered weakly through the gap in the blinds, casting a long stripe across the corner desk cluttered with notes and half-empty coffee cups. Franc Merlot sat hunched in his chair, fingers drumming against the smooth leather cover of the manifest. Outside, the hum of St. Petersburg's waking city felt distant, as if the town itself were holding its breath.

His phone buzzed, jolting him from a restless haze. Carly's name blinked on the screen.

"Any local leads?" the message read.

Franc tapped back a reply, his mind already turning over the pieces: the orchid's warning, the whispered threats, the mysterious shipment. The past wasn't done with him yet and Caldwell's shadow loomed larger than ever.

He rose and pulled open the drawer, fingers brushing over a faded photo pinned beneath a stack of papers. A vineyard bathed in twilight, the Château de Lirac standing proud and silent. Somewhere in that stillness lay the truth buried beneath layers of wine, money, and deceit.

Franc sank comfortably into his chair. The morning light was growing stronger, but clarity remained elusive.

He replayed the facts in his mind: the whispers in Bordeaux, the mysterious shipment, the orchid warning, and the shadows lurking at the marina.

What if Caldwell had orchestrated the entire saga to mislead them, buying time to disappear again?

The thought unsettled him, but there was no room for doubt now.

After a long pause and several sips from his fourth cup of strong black coffee, Franc reached for the phone and dialed room service from Paul's Landing, the pool side restaurant.

"I'll have the eggs benedict with blue crab meat, please," he said, voice steady but tired. "And a side of that hollandaise sauce you make here with rich, buttery toast, too. Thick-cut bacon, crisped just right, and a glass of your fresh squeezed Florida orange juice." When in Rome right, he thought and laughed to himself.

As he hung up, Franc allowed himself a brief smile. Even in the middle of a storm, some comforts were worth savoring.

He settled back in, ready to let his thoughts roam while the meal arrived. One way or another, today would bring answers. Or at least, new questions worth chasing.

The knock at the door was soft but precise, a contrast to the chaos swirling inside Franc's mind. He opened it to find the room service attendant balancing a tray with the carefully plated eggs benedict, the crab meat nestled beneath the perfectly poached eggs, a drizzle of hollandaise pooling beside the bacon and toast.

"Thank you," Franc said, closing the door behind him as the scent of butter and citrus filled the room.

He took his first bite slowly, the rich flavors grounding him for a moment. His eyes drifted back to the manifest lying on the desk. The crate from Bordeaux. The signature. The mysterious 'delivery' Sofia had whispered about. Each piece felt like a code, but whose code was it? And what was the message?

Franc's phone buzzed, a new email from Carly.

He opened it eagerly, scanning the brief message:

Still digging on the Cézanne. Found some oddities in the auction records - some suspicious transfers around the time Caldwell disappeared.

The words hit him hard. Carly's instincts matched his own doubts. It looked more like they were being led in circles again, while the real chase slipped through their fingers.

Frustrated, Franc leaned back, toast halfway to his mouth, and stared out the window at the shimmering marina below. The sun was rising, but the shadows remained. He was no stranger to obstacles, but this was something else where the stakes were hidden beneath layers of wealth, influence, and lies. Potentially dangerous layers.

He would call Carly soon, piece together what little they had, and figure out the next move. But first, he needed clarity. The kind only time and patience could provide.

For now, he ate.

Franc finished the last bite, setting his fork down with deliberate calm. The quiet clink against the plate was louder than he expected, breaking the stillness that had settled over him. He pushed the empty plate aside and rubbed his temples, the weight of uncertainty pressing in.

The more he thought about it, the more the pieces felt like a possible fraudulent lead, designed to busy them in another endless pursuit.

His phone buzzed again, this time a text message from Mike Delaney:

> *Meet me for coffee?*
> *Got some info you need to hear. Discreet.*

Franc hesitated. Mike had been helpful, but his connections were murky, and his loyalties unknown.

Still, if anyone had a thread to follow, it was Mike.

After a moment's pause, Franc typed back:

> *Meet me in the lobby in 30.*

He stood and walked to the window, gazing down at the marina where the first light of dawn cast long shadows across the water. The orchid on the desk, now wilted, seemed to mock him. Beautiful, fragile, and fading fast.

This wasn't just about art or money anymore.

But Franc Merlot had dug himself in with both feet.

The hotel lobby was quiet in the early morning haze, sunlight filtering through the tall glass windows and catching the dust motes in the air. Franc settled into a corner table near the small café, the scent of freshly ground beans mingling with the faint salt from the nearby bay. Mike Delaney arrived moments later, his usual easy smile tempered by a seriousness that didn't go unnoticed.

"Morning," Mike said, sliding into the seat across from Franc. "I owe you some answers."

Franc nodded, watching him carefully. "I'm listening."

Mike pulled a folded envelope from his jacket pocket, placing it on the table. "Caldwell's been busy. Not just with the gallery or Vinoy. There's more beneath the surface Contracts, offshore accounts, people moving money in ways that don't show up on normal ledgers."

Franc unfolded the envelope and pulled out a set of photocopied bank statements, coded transactions, and a few blurry security photos showing a late-night meeting near the docks.

"This isn't just art laundering," Mike said quietly. "There's talk of smuggling artifacts, documents, maybe worse. The Cézanne? It seems to have been a cover story. A distraction to keep you chasing shadows." But we'll confirm it.

Franc's eyes flicked up, his instincts confirming the doubt he'd felt alone in his room.

"Why tell me this now?" Franc asked.

Mike hesitated. "Because you're not just some curious outsider. And because, frankly, someone's been watching me, too."

Franc's jaw tightened. "Who?"

Mike shrugged. "Could be Caldwell's people. Could be the group of men behind him. Either way, you could use my help."

Franc folded the papers back into the envelope. "Then we need to figure out who's actually behind this. And fast."

Mike leaned in, voice low. "I know a place where we can start. But it's not in any ledger."

Franc's pulse quickened. "Lead the way."

The scents of blooming jasmine from nearby patios beautifully framed St. Petersburg, as they stepped out in search of a quick bite and to further elaborate on Mike's idea. Beneath the surface, Franc knew, old money and darker dealings stirred close by.

He pocketed the envelope Mike had handed him, the weight of its contents heavier than the papers themselves. Contracts and offshore accounts, coded transactions, blurry photos, possible clues to a hidden network that sprawled farther than he'd imagined. The Château de Lirac and Vinoy

Investment Partners were both threads woven into this tapestry of secrets.

Franc and Mike ventured across the street into a quaint coffee shop that served great quick food options called the Annex. Franc had frequently patronized it on early morning walks grabbing coffee to go.

Franc's phone buzzed, a message from Carly flashing on screen:

> *Any luck on the manifest?*

He typed back quickly:

> *More than luck. We're on the edge of something bigger. And Mike is here to help.*

After long discussions, Mike headed back north to Tampa as Franc went back to his room for a much needed, quick change of clothes and cleaned up before wrapping his daytime schedule for night.

As the evening settled in, Franc made his way over to Flute and Dram, a popular bar/restaurant with nightly live music nestled along Beach Drive. Its modern decor, outdoor atmosphere, and soft lighting under covered shelter, promised a nice refuge, and place to gather thoughts while planning his next move.

The hostess led him to a corner with a fire pit table and a magnificent view looking back over the distant lights of the marina. Franc ordered his usual glass of Bordeaux, the taste, a small comfort, while the waiter took his food order, his mind drifted back to the earlier conversation with Mike.

Contracts that didn't exist on paper. Money slipping through invisible channels. People watching, waiting. What had started as a search for a missing man and a stolen painting was now entrenched in a more serious game.

The waiter returned soon after setting down his plate, a wooden board of charcuterie. Franc picked at the cheese and food samples, but his mind was still elsewhere, circling the details Mike had revealed.

He pulled out his phone again and re-read the bank statements, the photos, the names. Each mere fragments, but whose picture would surely come into focus.

Franc knew one thing for certain, the night ahead wouldn't stay quiet.

Franc signaled the waiter for another glass of wine, settling in as he reached into his jacket pocket and pulled out a slender, Churchill-sized Davidoff cigar he had carefully selected from their humidor inside upon arriving earlier. It had become a nightly ritual since arriving in St. Petersburg. A small indulgence that grounded him amidst the chaos.

He cut the tip with his V-cutter and torch-lit the cigar with practiced ease, then drew in the rich, earthy smoke. The warm tendrils curled slowly upward as live music blared out over the crowd of people. The music was a welcome distraction, a balm for his restless mind.

Franc let his eyes wander over the growing crowds as couples strolling by hand in hand, tourists snapping photos, locals indulging in their preferred libations, weaving through the streets enjoying late night entertainment. Life moved on around him, vibrant and unaware of the undercurrents swirling beneath the surface.

For a moment, he allowed himself the luxury of detachment, savoring the blend of smoke, wine, and music. But even as the night air filled with musical notes and laughter, Franc's thoughts circled back to the tangled web of Caldwell, and his LLC companies.

The questions remained, relentless as ever.

Franc's gaze drifted beyond the sidewalk, past the swaying palms lining Beach Drive. Through the dark silhouette of Straub Park, just two blocks north, the Vinoy commanded attention, its stately lights piercing the night like a beacon.

The sight jolted him back to reality. The elegant ballroom, the whispered warnings, Sofia's fear. All of it was still very much alive, waiting just beyond the city's calm veneer.

The glow from the hotel seemed almost a challenge, a reminder that the night's puzzles weren't confined to shadows but played out under gilded chandeliers and polished tiled floors.

Franc took a slow drag from his cigar; the smoke exhaled into a cloud overhead. The game was far from over, and the heart of it was right there within those walls, beneath the sparkling lights.

He glanced back at the empty glass on his table, signaling the waiter for one last refill before he made his decision.

Tonight, the pieces were coming into focus. But the question remained: would he have the wherewithal to make sense of it all?

Nearing midnight, Franc glanced down at his watch. Carly would be stirring in Bordeaux by now, six hours ahead, likely just walking into her day. Their recent conversations had been limited to terse emails, a coded, careful, dance of information stretched across continents. He wanted to hear her voice, to bridge the distance with something real.

Finishing his wine, Franc stood, feeling the night's quiet presence settle around him like a cloak. The short walk back to the Vinoy felt laborious now, each step echoing with questions and half-truths.

Inside his room, immediately feeling the welcomed air conditioning, he closed the door and quickly settled under the cool sheets in bed. He pulled out his phone, scrolling briefly through their email chain, then dialed.

As the line rang, his mind drifted back to the afternoon, and his meeting with Mike Delaney. The attorney's polished charm, the subtle evasions, the way he skirted around Caldwell's name like it was a live wire. Mike was a man who navigated shadows with ease, but tonight Franc wondered just how much of the truth he'd been given.

The phone clicked, and Carly's voice came through, warm, familiar, but tinged with the distance of a thousand miles.

"Franc," she said softly.

He took a breath. "Carly, I'm back at my room ready to sleep but there's more here than I thought. Sofia is scared. I need to know - do you think the

Cézanne's really missing? Or are we being played?" Mike believes it was a cover.

Carly paused. "I've been checking. The trail's cold, but there are things that don't add up. Someone's feeding us pieces, but I'm not sure if it's to help or to trap us."

They spoke for nearly fifteen minutes, as Franc filled her in on the guys on the dock and the manifest.

Franc's fingers tightened around the phone. "And we have to be careful. I'm not walking blind into this, whatever game Caldwell's playing."

"Agreed," Carly said. "Keep your eyes open. And Franc, don't trust anyone, even Mike more than you need to."

The line went silent for a moment, then Carly's voice softened. "Call me when you're ready for me to join you there."

Franc nodded in approval, though she couldn't see him. "I will."

He hung up, the weight of the night pressing in. Tomorrow would bring more questions, and maybe a few answers. But for now, the silence of the Vinoy settled around him, full of whispers yet to be uncovered.

Chapter Eight

Crossing Lines

Carly set her phone down on the worn oak desk, the echo of Franc's voice lingering in the quiet room. Outside, the soft hum of Bordeaux morning seeped through the window, the distant clatter of trams, early footsteps stirred on cobblestones. But inside, the air felt heavier, charged with the weight of their conversation.

She ran a hand through her hair, the lines of worry etched deeper than they had been days ago. Franc's doubts mirrored her own. The missing Cézanne, the shadows trailing Caldwell's name, were they chasing a ghost, or had someone carefully crafted a trap to lead them astray?

A sudden thought took hold, sharp and insistent. If the trail was cold here, maybe it was heating up somewhere else. Nice. The city of sun, secrets, and stolen masterpieces. Carly pulled her laptop closer, fingers already typing "train schedules Bordeaux to Nice." The morning departures flashed up, promising a swift escape south.

She booked a ticket for the earliest train. As the confirmation pinged on her screen, Carly's eyes flicked to the faded map pinned to the wall, tracing the route from Bordeaux to the glittering coastline. She wasn't sure what awaited in Nice, but she knew she had to follow it.

Packing light, she grabbed her coat and tucked the train ticket into her pocket. There was no turning back now. Somewhere between vineyards and Mediterranean waves answers waited.

Bordeaux, France — The Same Morning

Carly exhaled, rubbing her eyes. Franc's words had confirmed, something far more intricate was at play. And now her instinct took over. The Cézanne… if it ever existed… if it ever vanished… Nice would be the place to find the truth.

Later That Morning — Nice

The sun spilled over the Mediterranean as Carly stepped from the train and into the heart of the Riviera. Before diving into her schedule, she stopped at the bustling market on Rue Bonaparte for a familiar comfort: espresso and a croissant, flaky and warm. She perched at a small table, watching locals barter over tomatoes and flowers, anchoring herself before what she hoped would be a revelatory day.

Her first meeting was at Galerie de l'Écume, where Martine Delaye greeted her with polite skepticism. "Missing Cézanne?" Martine arched an eyebrow. "People have been 'missing' Cézannes for decades."

But not this one.

Martine admitted some discreet inquiries had come through, post-impressionist, anonymous, hush-hush. "No one names names," she said, "but collectors are curious again. That usually means something is moving."

It wasn't much, but it was a crack.

Carly stepped out of the gallery with the sea air in her lungs and Pascal Renaud's name in her sights. He had agreed to meet at a restaurant along the Promenade des Anglais that evening. Once a registrar for the Musée Matisse, now something more elusive, Pascal operated in the twilight between provenance and profit.

She didn't know what he would say. But if anyone could track the whereabouts of a painting smuggled from Bordeaux, it would be Pascal.

And if he confirmed her hunch?

Then it meant Franc was right to worry, and far from being played, they might have been getting too close all along.

Carly wandered through the sun-warmed streets of Nice, weaving past shuttered antique shops and pastel-painted buildings that leaned in close like old friends trading secrets. The city was, as she remembered, alive with color, movement, and an undercurrent of Mediterranean ease. But her mind was sharp, scanning every storefront and gallery window with a purpose.

She wasn't here to soak in charm. She was here for answers.

Turning off a busy boulevard, she found her way to a small boutique hotel tucked behind an olive tree–lined courtyard. The woman at the front desk greeted her warmly in accented English and handed over the room key, a real one, not a plastic card. Carly smiled at the detail.

In her room, she opened the windows to let the sea breeze cut through the faint scent of travel and tension. She sat for a moment on the edge of the bed, kicking off her shoes and letting the silence settle in. Her phone buzzed with an email from

Franc, just a note:

Let me know how it goes. Be safe.

She didn't answer. Not yet.

Instead, she unpacked and laid out a navy dress for dinner. Simple, confident. The kind of thing she wore when she needed to command respect without saying a word. She set it aside and stepped into the bathroom, splashing cold water on her face. The mirror reflected someone who looked rested but weary, someone who had started the day chasing a missing Cézanne but now believed the trail had been a farce all along.

Because if Pascal's inclination was right and she trusted his gut as much as her own, there was no stolen Cézanne. There may never have been. The entire mystery had been crafted with precision. A ruse. Somehow Mike had discovered it was a mere cover story as well, according to Franc's phone call.

Carly stood at the window; arms folded across her chest. The trip to Nice hadn't been for nothing. It could give her closure, confirmation that her instincts hadn't betrayed her. The Cézanne story had been the perfect distraction. Clean. Intriguing.

Valuable. But its purpose wasn't to be found. It was to send people like her, and Franc, on a curated wild goose chase while something else, something real, slipped by unnoticed.

Maybe the real question now wasn't what had been stolen.

It was: Why the distraction. What was being hidden?

She looked down at her watch. Two hours until her dinner with Pascal and the truth once and for all.

She would need to be careful. And she'd need to be certain she wasn't walking into a second misdirection.

But first, she'd enjoy a glass of wine on the terrace. After all, even in the pursuit of truth, some rituals were worth keeping.

The restaurant was tucked just off the Promenade des Anglais, where the last blush of daylight still clung to the sea. Pascal had chosen well. It was elegant without being ostentatious, white linen, flickering candles, and a terrace that offered both privacy and the vibe of the Mediterranean night.

Carly arrived precisely on time. Pascal was already seated, a glass of chilled Sancerre in hand, his phone face down beside the silverware.

"Carly," he stood, offering the familiar kiss to each cheek. "You look like you've had a long day."

She gave him a tired smile. "That bad?" She joked. "A long few months, actually."

They ordered quickly, her grilled octopus with lemon-thyme butter, Pascal the duck confit, and settled into the kind of quiet that only came between two people who had chased enough ghosts to recognize the toll. When the first course arrived, Pascal finally spoke.

"I didn't want to put this in writing. And certainly not prematurely." he began, slicing his foie gras slowly, methodically. "Not in an email. Not on the phone. Too many things, too many names are being watched."

Carly leaned in. "So, it's not just us imagining shadows."

"No. But the Cézanne is definitely a lie." He said it plainly, without hesitation. "I've confirmed it."

"How?"

Pascal took a sip of wine, then met her gaze. "I spoke with two curators, one in Paris, one in Bern, and someone who owes me a favor in Zurich. No red flags in the last five years. No private transactions gone dark, no insurance claims hidden from public view. And the art piece Caldwell was supposedly asking about? It was sold legally fifteen years ago. It hasn't moved since. It's hanging in a villa in Florence, still in the possession of the same family. I confirmed with photographic proof."

Carly felt the truth settle over her like a stone.

"So, all of this…" she said slowly, "was a way to get us looking in the wrong place."

Pascal nodded. "You were meant to chase provenance records and collectors in the shadows. But the real activity, whatever it is, has nothing to do with Cézanne. That part was designed to catch your interest. Or distract you from something more delicate."

Carly stirred her wine absently. "Franc will need to hear this."

"I know. That's why I agreed to meet. I trust him. But I trust you more." Pascal's voice softened. "Whoever planted this story knew you both couldn't resist a puzzle like this. They used that."

"And Caldwell?" Carly asked. "Was he in on it?"

"I believe so. The timing lines up. He vanished when the Cézanne rumors started. Now he resurfaces, conveniently, just as the painting trail dries up."

Their entrées arrived. Carly barely touched hers.

Pascal reached across the table and placed his hand gently over hers. "You were never meant to find a painting. You were meant to believe one was missing. And now that we know the truth, we have to ask, what were they really moving from Bordeaux to Florida?"

Carly nodded, the full weight of it sinking in. "It's time to go deeper."

Pascal smiled, but it didn't reach his eyes. "Just be careful, Carly. They've already misled you once. They won't hesitate to do worse next time."

She looked out toward the glittering sea, the sound of waves brushing against the shore. For the first time since arriving in Nice, she felt clear. The distraction had done its job, but it was over now.

The real mystery lay ahead.

And she was done chasing ghosts.

Chapter Nine

Smoke and Signals

The morning haze along Beach Drive shimmered in the early light, casting long shadows from the banyan trees lining Straub Park. Franc Merlot stirred his coffee absently, seated at a corner table outside Cassis, the café's quiet buzz just enough to keep him grounded. The faint sting of sea air mixed with the citrus scent of freshly peeled orange rind from the table beside him.

His thoughts were less tranquil.

The meeting with Mike the night before had offered little comfort, too many evasions, too much guarded language. Mike hadn't lied, but he'd danced around Caldwell's name like a man defusing a landmine.

"He's back," Mike had said, nursing a scotch with the precision of someone who needed something to do with his hands. "But not the same man. He's playing in deeper waters now, Franc. He's not just buying art anymore, he's managing people. Dangerous ones."

That phrase clung to Franc like damp linen: managing people.

He sipped his coffee, but his appetite was gone. Last night's cigar still lingered on his palate, and the buzz of pedestrians warming up the sidewalk felt more invasive than charming. He pulled his notebook from his blazer pocket and scanned the pages, names, dates, and a scribbled reference to the shipping manifest Sofia had given him.

Aurora's Promise → Bordeaux crate → Sunlit Canvas → Central Ave.

Everything pointed to the same question: what was *really* in that crate?

His phone buzzed.

One new message.
From: Carly Leroux
Subject: Nice was a dead end, sort of.

Franc opened it immediately.

Carly's email:

> *Franc -*
>
> *The Cézanne isn't missing. Not even close. Pascal confirmed it. Verified ownership, current location, even recent high-res photos. The painting's in Florence and hasn't moved in over a decade.*
>
> *You were right to trust your instincts, but the trail we were chasing? A fabrication. The missing Cézanne was never the point.*
>
> *Someone wanted us distracted. Probably Caldwell. Maybe someone higher up. But here's the thing - Pascal thinks the timing of Caldwell's questions about*

vineyard family holdings in Bordeaux lines up with a very different sort of laundering operation. Real estate? Possibly. But it's the art angle that's used as the smoke screen.

Forget the Cézanne. Start asking what was in that crate from Château de Lirac. And look closer at Sunlit Canvas. It's more than a gallery. Pascal suspects it might be a staging ground, for what, he's not sure. But he's worried. And when Pascal's worried, so am I.

I'll be back in Bordeaux for a day or two, but I'm not done with this yet. Let's talk soon.

- Carly

Franc leaned back in his chair, staring past the row of palm trees toward the water. His fingers drummed the table. Carly's tone was sharp and focused. She wasn't just passing information along. She was warning him.

The Cézanne had been bait.

So, what, then, was the real prize?

He pulled his phone closer and opened his calendar. There was one name Mike had dropped casually last night over dinner. A man with a reputation for moving high-value assets through shell galleries.

And he had a known connection with Vinoy Investment Partners.

Franc closed the notebook and tossed a twenty on the table. As he stepped onto the sunlit sidewalk, he didn't feel lost anymore.

He felt like a fuse had been lit.

The Sunlit Canvas Gallery didn't look like a front for anything illicit. It was bright, clean, and disarmingly curated, white walls, track lighting, local artwork priced high enough to deter casual shoppers. An older woman, with a platinum pixie cut and smart navy jumpsuit, manned the reception desk. Franc walked in slow, hands in his blazer pockets, his expression casual.

He pretended to be his first visit to the gallery, admiring a painting of a surreal Florida mangrove as he scoped the place.

The interior had two main rooms. One forward-facing, with polished concrete floors and a small register. The second, more interesting, lay behind a floating wall panel, housing larger installations. Franc noted the locked door toward the back, unmarked, and tucked next to a narrow hallway likely leading to the office and storage.

The receptionist looked up. "Interested in anything specific?"

"Just browsing," Franc replied. "My girlfriend's into coastal art. I figured I'd surprise her."

She smiled professionally. "We rotate in new works every Friday. Today's shipment came in late last night from a private estate. Some Bordeaux pieces, figurative landscapes."

Franc nodded, hiding the flicker in his eyes. "Sounds fancy."

"It is. That crate's still in the back, actually, hadn't even made it to inventory this morning."

"Estate in Bordeaux, you said?"

She hesitated. "That's what the paperwork said. It came in through Vinoy Investment Partners, but most of our international deals go through them."

There it was.

Franc's mind snapped into place. They weren't hiding it. The gallery was laundering provenance; legitimizing select shipments with forged backstories. The receptionist believed she was selling art. But someone else had crafted the illusion.

He smiled again and drifted through the second room. Near the rear wall, he spotted something that didn't fit - a freestanding wooden crate, only partially opened. It wasn't just tall, it was deep, reinforced like a shipping container, not standard art packaging.

Too large for a painting.

He approached, tilting his head at a stylized vineyard scene hanging beside it.

"Is this from the new Bordeaux collection too?" he asked casually.

She followed his gaze. "Yes. That one's already priced at $14,000. I think it's... Château de Lirac?"

The same name from the manifest.

Bingo.

Franc nodded, offering a small whistle of appreciation, then slowly made his way back toward the exit.

"I'll think about it," he said with a casual wave. "Might bring her by later."

As he stepped into the St. Pete sun again, his mind was already sprinting.

The crate was here. It had come through the right pipeline. But it wasn't a painting - at least not only that. And whoever had orchestrated it was using Sunlit Canvas as a legitimate front to tuck something into plain sight.

The question now wasn't *if* this was bigger than a forged Cézanne.

It was, *how* much bigger?

He slipped on his sunglasses, walking with purpose now. He needed to find Sofia again and talk to the man Mike had hinted at last night.

Someone named Tomas Juric.

A financier. And, according to Mike, "the real brain behind Caldwell's second act."

Franc stepped into the shade of an overhang near the edge of Beach Drive, pulling out his phone and scrolling to Sofia's number. The last message she'd sent two nights ago still lingered unanswered. Just two words:

> *Be careful.*

He typed quickly:

> *You ok? Can We Meet? It's important. Something big is moving soon.*

He hesitated, then hit send.

Sofia was scared, no doubt still feeling the heat from the night on the docks. But Franc needed her. She had access. Eyes on the inside. She might've seen

Juric or known how Caldwell communicated when he didn't want to be found.

The name "Tomas Juric" kept looping through Franc's thoughts like an unsolved equation. Mike hadn't said much, just that Juric had once been an art consultant who morphed into something more elusive. Wealth manager, shell architect, clean-up man. Franc hadn't recognized the name in Bordeaux, but here in St. Pete, the trails were thinner, quieter. Juric was a man who left no digital fingerprint behind.

Franc ducked into a quiet wine bar near the marina, found a table in the back, and ordered a double espresso. He slid his laptop from his satchel, booting it up with a silent prayer that Carly's earlier email would yield something more.

She'd responded that morning.

> *Likely Caldwell. He wanted noise in France while something else moved through Florida. Watch the gallery. And the shell companies tied to Vinoy Investment Partners. One name kept surfacing in whispers: Tomas Juric. Can't pin*

him. But he's not new to this game. If he's there, you're close.

Franc scrolled through the gallery's LLC registration filings, then cross-referenced them with recent real estate trusts in the downtown corridor. Most were dead ends or generic investment vehicles.

But one hit made him pause: a limited partnership; Sapphire Docks Holdings. They own a property right near the marina, filed under a legal rep from Zagreb.

Zagreb. Croatian.

Juric.

Franc leaned back, heart rate ticking up. If Juric was staying anywhere, it was probably under an alias and if the Vinoy was too exposed, the condos at Sapphire Docks offered both privacy and a view of the gallery and marina.

He fired off another text to Sofia:

Think I found something. Near the marina. Can we talk? Tonight? Your place or somewhere safe. Let me know.

No answer.

He stared at the screen, sipping his espresso.

If Juric was who he suspected, the man wasn't just laundering Caldwell's assets. He was moving something whether it was money, art, or something, but what? The false trail in France was deliberate. Carly had sniffed it out. Now it was up to Franc to prove what the real objective had been.

He closed the laptop and rose; eyes set on the marina district.

If he couldn't find Juric face to face, he'd start by circling his probable lair. Tonight, he'd walk the perimeter of Sapphire Docks, see who came and went, and maybe, just maybe, intercept a ghost.

Chapter Ten

Demens Landing

The night air was dense with salt and stillness, the kind that clung to the skin and dampened sound. Franc retraced his steps along the marina, his shoes whispering against the weathered planks. The moon hung low, refracted in thin ripples across the water like a secret it refused to fully reveal.

He passed the row of now familiar yachts, like sentinels that never spoke, then slowly followed the gentle curve of the dock toward the bridge that arched over the marina's inlet. A battered municipal sign caught his eye, half-lit by a flickering lamp post: *Demens Landing.*

Franc paused, letting the name settle in.
"Fitting," he murmured to himself, lips curling into a dry half-smile. He'd landed here too, although not quite by design. The name, with its hint of destiny or undoing, carried the kind of poetic weight he'd learned not to ignore.

As he crossed the bridge, the water beneath was still, reflecting shadows of boats and palm fronds overhead. On the far side, he turned left, slipping into the tree-lined park that buffered the marina from the condo complexes beyond. He kept one eye on the path ahead, the other scanning the darkened balconies of Sapphire Docks, looming just beyond a thin stretch of road.

If Tomas Juric was there, he'd be well protected. Men like him didn't sleep in penthouses without cameras and layers of legal firepower. But even a ghost left footprints. Deliveries. Maintenance visits. Strange visitors arriving after hours. Franc watched, waited.

The wind stirred gently through the oaks, their limbs brushing like conspirators. A jogger passed by, headphones in, oblivious. Somewhere behind him, a gull squawked over a discarded food wrapper near a bench.

Franc's phone buzzed softly.

He pulled it from his pocket with restrained urgency, but it wasn't Sofia.

Carly:

> *Confirmed Juric was involved in a major laundering case tied to Monaco galleries back in 2018. All sealed now. Same pattern: shell corporations, fake valuations, temporary exhibitions. If he has resurfaced in St. Pete, Caldwell's plan is much larger than we thought.*

Franc exhaled slowly, eyes lifting toward the lights glowing from a third-story window at Sapphire Docks. Someone was home. Someone who didn't want to be seen.

He texted Carly back:

Watching now. Gallery is the pivot. But I'm betting Juric is the hinge. Stay close.

Then, switching to another thread, he tried again:

Sofia. It's me. Just need five minutes. Meet me where we first spoke. You're not safe until we talk.

Still no response.

But he didn't leave. He leaned against the base of a palm, watching. Waiting. Listening to the marina breathe. If this was the landing, he intended to make it count.

One way or another, someone would slip up, and Franc would be there when they did.

Sofia stared at the screen of her phone, its soft glow casting pale light across her dim apartment. The message from Franc sat there, waiting, no pressure in the words, but urgency in the silence between them.

Sofia. It's me. Just need five minutes. Meet me where we first spoke. You're not safe until we talk.

She looked up, eyes scanning the shadows dancing along her ceiling. The whisper of water from the small fountain outside her balcony was usually soothing. Tonight, it felt like a clock ticking down.

Her fingers hovered over the keyboard. She hadn't answered his last two messages. Not because she didn't want to, but people were watching. Her phone, her building, maybe even her.

But something shifted when she read his words this time.

You're not safe until we talk.

He wasn't wrong. Since slipping the manifest into his hands, Sofia had noticed more than just sideways glances. Someone had knocked on her door yesterday, late. No one was there when she looked through the peephole, but she hadn't imagined the soft footsteps walking away.

Franc had stood by her yacht that night like he belonged to this world of secrets. Calm. Sharp. Not reckless, but precise. And he listened.

She tapped out a reply, each word a decision.

Okay. One hour. Same place. Don't bring anyone.

She hit send and stood slowly, stretching the tension from her shoulders. Her hoodie lay crumpled on a nearby chair. She pulled it on, zipped it halfway, and tied her hair back tight. No earrings. No purse. Just her ID and phone.

In the hallway mirror, she barely recognized herself.

But it was time.

The only way out was through.

Franc's phone buzzed in his pocket just as he paused at the edge of Demens Landing, the faint breeze off the bay stirring his collar. He pulled it free and read the message, his breath catching slightly.

Okay. One hour. Same place. Don't bring anyone.

A small wave of relief washed through him. She had answered. He'd half-feared the silence meant something had happened, or that she'd vanished like Caldwell once did. He turned slowly and stared across the marina, back toward the dock where they'd met under the hush of moonlight. Somewhere in those creaking shadows, the next breadcrumb waited.

But as he slid the phone back into his jacket, something shifted.

A figure on the opposite dock.

Franc froze. Not because the man was watching him, he wasn't. In fact, he was too still. Facing the water, arms resting on the railing, as if he'd been standing there for some time. But it was the jacket that caught Franc's eye.

Light tan. Tailored. Familiar.

Just like Caldwell's.

Franc's stomach tightened. Could it be?

He stepped back toward the edge of the bridge, using the palm fronds for partial cover. The angle wasn't great, but he caught a glimpse of the man's profile, clean-shaven, mid-50s, sharp jawline. Definitely not a dockhand. But then...

The man turned slightly… and began to laugh. Talking to someone on a Bluetooth earpiece.

Not Caldwell.

Or at least not the Caldwell he remembered.

Franc exhaled, half-frustrated, half-relieved. Another false flag in a city that was starting to feel like it ran on them.

Still, something felt wrong. The man's posture was rehearsed, too composed. And he wasn't just standing by any boat. It was Aurora's Promise.

Franc's pulse quickened. No coincidence.

He took a photo from behind a tree, cropping out the man's face but capturing the back of the yacht and the timestamp. Just in case. As he did, his phone buzzed again.

Unknown number.

He hesitated, then answered.

A voice on the line, low and clipped. "If you're smart, you'll stop asking about Juric. And you'll stay away from the girl."

Click.

Franc stared at the phone. His finger hovered over redial, but there was no number.

His jaw tightened.

He turned back toward the direction of the meeting spot, heart steady now, senses sharp.

If someone was warning him off, it meant he was close.

Chapter Eleven

A Sip of Silence

Carly adjusted her sunglasses as she settled into her
usual corner table at Le Chapon Fin, one of
Bordeaux's oldest and most elegantly preserved
dining rooms. The vaulted ceiling of carved stone
gave the illusion of a limestone grotto, cool and
serene, a stark contrast to the whirlwind of her week.
A tall window framed the sun-dappled street
beyond, filtering in light that danced across her wine
glass.

She sipped a chilled glass of Sémillon and reviewed notes on her phone, half-distracted as her starter arrived. Duck foie gras with fig chutney and toasted brioche. The richness of the dish pulled her attention back to the present, to the sanctuary of her surroundings. Bordeaux might have been tangled in ghosts and shadows lately, but here, in this moment, it was still hers. A city of refinement, of careful indulgence. And when she allowed herself, it was a haven.

Additional calls from prior inquiries had come in that morning, two gallery owners, a private appraiser in Marseilles, and a quietly worded inquiry from a familiar name in Paris's art restitution circle. Each confirmed what Pascal had made clear: there was no active registry, alert, or trace of a missing Cézanne in any current European records. She deleted the voicemails, having already gained the information earlier from Pascal.

Carly paused and breathed in the aroma, the weight of her thoughts melting just enough to let her enjoy the bite. It was one of her quiet luxuries: Knowing when to allow peace a seat at the table.

But only for a moment.

She reached for her phone again, opening her encrypted email and composing a message to Franc.

She hesitated, then typed a message.

This one a simple text.

Having dinner. Let's talk soon.

She set her phone down, this time not to pick it up again. The dessert menu was placed in front of her, and she nodded politely. She'd skip it. There were too many flavors already stirring in her mind.

Outside, the narrow streets of Bordeaux gleamed under the afternoon sun. Carly took one last sip of wine, then tucked her notepad into her bag and stood to leave. Nice had offered closure. Bordeaux was recalibrating. And now her attention turned fully toward Florida.

Later That Day — St. Petersburg, Florida

Franc leaned against the shaded balcony railing of his suite at the Vinoy, the phone pressed to his ear as he looked out across the marina. The sunlight sparkled on the water, a jarring contrast to the conversation he was about to have. He rubbed the bridge of his nose, exhausted but alert.

Carly picked up on the third ring.

"Bonjour," she said, her voice warm and steady. "I was beginning to wonder if I'd have to fly back and rattle you awake."

Franc smiled faintly. "You'd probably enjoy that too much."

"I would. Now talk to me. I got your text. 'Crazy night.' That's all you wrote."

"Yeah," he exhaled, walking back inside and sitting on the arm of the leather chair. "That was the short version."

He recounted the previous evening, starting with his walk through Demens Landing, the view of the Vinoy from across Straub Park, and then Sofia's sudden agreement to meet. Carly listened in silence as he detailed the encounter: Sofia's urgency, her subtle glances toward the water, the way she spoke like someone being watched even when no one was around.

"She didn't bring much," Franc said. "But her fear said more than her words. There's something in that yacht's movements. Aurora's Promise. She said Caldwell was aboard days ago, meeting someone. Something about a delivery again."

"Another shipment?" Carly asked.

"Maybe. She didn't see it directly. But she heard him mention timelines, discretion and my name. Again."

Carly paused. "Then he knows you're on his trail. And he wants you to know he knows."

"Exactly, just enough to make noise but not enough to show his hand."

There was a silence between them.

"I read your email," Franc continued. "Back to square one."

"Not quite," Carly said. "It means we stop chasing what they want us to chase. It means we start looking at what they're hiding."

Franc let the thought settle. "And if Sofia's right… Caldwell's not hiding stolen paintings. He's moving something else. Or someone."

Another pause. Carly's voice softened. "Do you trust her?"

"I want to, but she was vague and brief, to say the least." Franc admitted. "But fear can be genuine even when the facts aren't. She might be playing her own game."

There was the clink of a glass on her end, then a long breath. "Alright, here's what I'm thinking," Carly said. "I fly out. Give me forty-eight hours to settle things here, and I'll meet you in St. Pete. We'll crack this together."

Franc smiled, leaning back in the chair. "You just miss the humidity."

"I miss being in the room when the clues drop. And maybe," she added, "I miss our pace too."

He chuckled. "Pack light. This city's sunshine doesn't play fair."

They stayed on the line a few moments longer, small talk, no strategy, no tension. Just the comfort of being back in sync.

After they hung up, Franc stood by the window again. Across the way, Aurora's Promise sat at dock, still and gleaming in the sunlight like a beast at rest.

But he knew better.

Something moved beneath that stillness.

And with Carly arriving soon, they would move, too.

Morning Veranda

Franc sat at a small marble-topped table on the front veranda of the Vinoy, the morning light spilling gently over the white columns and pink stucco walls. The shade from the awning kept the rising heat at bay, and the gentle clink of breakfast silverware and murmured conversations around him created a pleasant hum of life. He nursed his first cup of coffee, eyes drifting between the luxury cars rolling up Beach Drive and the slow rhythm of palm fronds and blue sky overhead.

A couple seated near him appeared to be Midwestern, by the accent as they chatted amiably about dolphin tours and Sunday brunch spots. Another pair of women, sun-hatted and sipping mimosas, debated whether to visit the Dali Museum or spend the day shopping on Central.

Franc offered a few polite smiles, nodding occasionally when conversation floated his way. He had long ago learned to blend into the relaxed tempo of hotel life when needed. He even enjoyed the charade, pretending, if only for a moment, that he was just another traveler enjoying Florida's charm, not a man unwinding a knot of international deceit.

"More coffee, Mr. Merlot?"

Franc looked up, catching the warm smile of Gina, the server who had brought him coffee every morning that week. Her dark hair was pulled into a neat braid, and her eyes had that familiar brightness of someone who saw dozens of people a day but still remembered the ones who tipped in conversation as well as cash.

"Always, Gina. And thank you," he said, lifting his cup slightly.

She poured, expertly, without a drop spilled. "Another busy day?"

Franc gave a half smile. "That depends who's asking."

Gina laughed. "Just making sure you get properly caffeinated for whatever adventure awaits. Some guests are heading to the beach… others? Just escaping life."

Franc nodded at that. "Sometimes they're one and the same."

As she moved on to another table, Franc leaned back in his chair, letting the coffee settle into his system. There was a comfort to this place, the lazy elegance of the veranda, the way strangers could become brief companions over shared sunrises and pastries. He let himself sink into the illusion for a moment longer.

But reality tugged at the edges of his mind.

He wasn't here for rest or rebirth. Not yet.

As lovely as this corner of St. Petersburg was, as much as he could see himself sinking into its rhythm someday, he had questions to answer, shadows to expose. And now with Carly on her way and Sofia's uneasy warning still fresh, he felt the pieces shifting again.

He pulled out his phone and glanced at his messages.

Nothing from Sofia yet. Nothing from Tomas either.

He set the cup down, exhaled slowly, and turned his attention inward, replaying the last conversation with Sofia, dissecting the tone, the fear, the uncertainty. And the name Tomas Juric continued to echo.

Something in that name still didn't sit right.

Franc took his last sip of coffee, letting the moment stretch. The warmth grounded him. Rising to leave, he'd barely tuned into the group of men at the far end of the veranda until he caught a few key words:

"…usual tee time, one o'clock, same foursome, maybe that new guy will join today…"

"Vinoy course is in great shape after the rain."

Golf.

Franc's eyes lifted slightly, casual but alert. The men were older, well-groomed, their polos and pastel shorts the uniform of leisure but their voices held a certain tone. Not arrogance exactly, but of comfort and confidence. These weren't tourists. These were locals. Regulars.

He leaned back, stretching slightly, mind kicking up a gear.

Golf… at the Vinoy Club. Snell Isle.

Of course.

Sometimes proximity breeds clarity. What if the pattern he was chasing wasn't just in art or forged documents, but in habits? In membership lists? Who shows up, week after week, confident they're never watched?

He reached for his phone and quickly scrolled to Mike's number. The phone rang once, twice, and then,

"Franc. What's up?"

"Morning," Franc said, watching the men rise to leave. "You ever play the Vinoy Club golf course?"

There was a pause. "Snell Isle? Sure, a couple times a year when I can sneak out. Why?"

"I'm thinking of shaking up the day. Got some energy I need to put somewhere. Are you interested in a round this afternoon?"

Mike chuckled. "You, playing golf? This must be serious."

"It is," Franc said evenly. "But I'm hoping it doesn't feel like it."

Mike caught the undertone. "Are you expecting to find something out there?"

"I'm not sure. Maybe nothing. Maybe something someone says or doesn't say. I just think getting out of this loop, same streets, same gallery doors, same marina shadows. It might shift something."

A moment of silence.

Then Mike answered, "Call the pro shop and get us a tee time. Are you picking me up or meeting me there?"

"I'll drive. I'll text you after I confirm."

They hung up, his pulse steady but his mind was racing. He tipped Gina a twenty, nodded his thanks, and left.

Golf might not be an obvious move, but then again, he'd always known the truth didn't like straight lines.

It liked fairways, clubhouses, and the illusion of harmless pastimes.

He walked inside to arrange a rental set of clubs and texted Mike the time.

Today, the game would be more than sport.

Back in his suite, Franc stared at the open closet. He wasn't sure if it was the Florida heat or the idea of eighteen holes with borrowed clubs, but he already felt out of rhythm. Golf had never been his domain. He preferred sharp suits and sharper instincts, things that held up in tense conversations, not sand traps. Still, he buttoned a crisp collared shirt, slipped on lightweight slacks, and nodded to his reflection. He looked the part. That would have to be enough.

As he packed a few essentials in a small leather satchel, scanning his memory for oversights; phone charger, notepad, sunglasses. His mind shifted to Carly. By this time tomorrow, she'd be helping, working beside him again, in the middle of this twisted story that kept stretching across oceans. A welcome complication, he thought. Maybe even a necessary one.

He lifted his phone and called her.

Straight to voicemail.

He smiled at the recording tone, visualizing her somewhere in Bordeaux, pacing or writing or double-checking her carry-on list.

"Hey, it's me. Just wanted to say I'm thinking about you and I'm looking forward to having you here. I'll be at the airport in the morning. I've got a loaner from the hotel, so I'll drive over to Tampa and meet you. I'll keep an eye on the flight info, make sure everything's on time."

He hesitated for half a breath, then softened his voice.

"Travel safe, Carly. I'll see you soon."

He hung up, the message feeling incomplete in all the right ways.

There was too much to say, too much they'd say face to face.

Franc grabbed his sunglasses, slipped them on, and headed down to the valet to pick up the sleek silver loaner Mercedes the hotel had arranged. He offered a nod of thanks, took the keys, and slid into the driver's seat.

Tee times waited, and he wasn't sure whether he was heading into a relaxed afternoon or the beginning of something far more telling.

Chapter Twelve

The Weight of Silence

Sofia sat at a window table inside a coffee shop; her fingers wrapped around a ceramic mug that had long gone cold. Outside, the breeze carried the scent of salt and jasmine through the open door, but inside her mind, things were anything but light. She hadn't slept much. Every knock on the wall, every creak of her apartment floor above the marina, felt like a reminder: she had crossed a line.

Across the table, a woman in her mid-fifties stirred honey into tea, her face drawn but calm. Lucienne Roche. Not her real name, Sofia guessed, but she'd never asked. They had met under tense circumstances months ago, when Sofia's work at Sunlit Canvas intersected with something she shouldn't have seen. Since then, Lucienne had become her lifeline, her informant, and her warning bell.

"I don't like that you met with him," Lucienne said without preamble, voice quiet but firm. "You don't know what Merlot's chasing."

Sofia leaned back, eyes scanning the morning crowd of laptop-lit tables and casual tourists. "He's smarter than they give him credit for, but if I hadn't warned him, he'd be a headline by now."

"That may still happen," Lucienne said, tapping her spoon once before setting it down. "This isn't just about Caldwell anymore. There's pressure coming in from Monaco. Old favors. People who don't like exposure."

Sofia felt the tension behind her eyes. "He's already locked in. I might be, too."

Lucienne nodded slowly. "And yet you're still helping him."

There was no judgment in her tone, only observation.

Sofia looked down into her mug. "He asked the right questions. That's rare around here."

A silence stretched between them, heavy with implication. Finally, Lucienne pulled a small envelope from her leather bag and slid it across the table.

"This is the name you wanted. The one who processed that Bordeaux shipment through Vinoy Investments. It's not Caldwell, he's just the face. This man runs the paperwork, the logistics, the ghost paths. I suggest you give it to your friend and disappear."

Sofia picked it up without opening it, tucking it into her jacket. "Not yet. Not until I'm sure what Caldwell's hiding."

Lucienne sighed and stood, gathering her things. "Be careful, Sofia. You think you're walking a line, but you're already off it."

As Lucienne vanished into the St. Pete morning, Sofia remained seated, heart rate accelerated, eyes on the doorway.

She would text Franc soon, maybe. But for now, she needed to see something for herself.

She stood, pocketed the envelope, and stepped into the light.

She had an appointment at a private studio that evening. One tied to a forgotten artist, a forged signature, and a connection that might unravel more than she intended.

Chapter Thirteen

Fairways and Greens

Mike's truck eased to a stop in front of Vinoy's entrance, the late-morning sun glinting off its polished hood. Franc stepped out from beneath the shaded veranda, his crisp white shirt catching the light like a sail. Slacks pressed, shoes shined. He looked more prepared for a board meeting than a round of golf.

Mike chuckled as he leaned across to push the passenger door open. "You're aware we're not playing at Augusta National, right?"

Franc slid in, adjusting his collar. "Relax. I plan to pick up a real golf shirt at the pro shop. I didn't exactly come to Florida with golf in mind."

"Clearly," Mike said, putting the truck into gear and pulling away from the hotel. "You planning to play in loafers, too?"

Franc smirked. "I'm adaptable. Besides, the objective isn't a perfect swing, it's a change of scenery. And possibly a conversation overheard in the cart behind us."

Mike gave him a side glance. "More leads, I'm guessing?"

Franc looked out at the water in Coffee Pot Bayou as they crossed the bridge toward Snell Isle. "Less ghosts, more threads. Sofia confirmed something's moving under the surface, and if Caldwell's front is as fragile as it feels, someone around here knows. Golf courses attract deals."

Mike nodded. "And rich men loosen up after the ninth hole."

"Exactly."

They rode in companionable silence for a moment, the city falling behind them. As they reached the Vinoy Golf Club's gated entrance, Franc leaned forward, taking in the neat rows of palm trees and the polished signage. It was a Florida he rarely indulged in, the curated tranquility, the slow pace, the illusion of control. It was no wonder those who could, retired here or called it a second home.

They parked in a spot nearest the clubhouse, where music played softly from hidden speakers and golf carts buzzed in quiet procession. A young man, polite and professional, pulled up behind Mike's truck to welcome them and take their bags.

"Go get your uniform," Mike said, nodding toward the pro shop entrance. "I'll get us checked in."

Franc walked in under the copper awning, the sudden chill of air conditioning met him like a wall. Apparel and assorted sets of golf clubs lined the walls with surgical precision, each color-coded and branded with embroidered logos. He browsed quickly, settled on a pale blue Vinoy-branded shirt, and ducked into the fitting room to change. As he adjusted the collar and stepped out, he caught his own reflection in the mirror.

He smiled, in approval of his new purchase, yet the sense that even here, in a place designed for leisure, the chase followed him. But he pushed the thought down and returned to Mike, waiting with a cart already loaded and ready to proceed to the first tee.

"You clean up okay," Mike said. "Now let's see if that European poise translates to your swing."

Franc grinned. "You may regret this invitation."

They rolled up to the tee box, the smell of cut grass and distant cigars already in the air. But even as the golf balls flew and pleasantries were exchanged with two other players joining their group, Franc kept his ears open listening for names, deals, locations. Any sign that someone, somewhere, knew more than he did.

By the fifth hole, Franc was beginning to feel more like a golf spectator than a participant. His swing lacked rhythm, but his instincts remained sharp. The course itself was lush and sprawling across the quiet elegance of Snell Isle, offering more than just scenery. It offered people and relationships.

Mike had already slipped comfortably into the rhythm of the game, offering pointers when appropriate but mostly letting Franc observe. Their playing partners, Wes and Clark, were pleasant, polished corporate types with just enough swagger to show they belonged.

The small talk flowed easily. Business chatter, local restaurant favorites, a complaint about a new condo development choking the skyline, it was all light, just noise on the fairway. But Franc paid attention.

Wes, in a soft baby-blue quarter-zip, mentioned he'd been at the Vinoy last weekend for a fundraiser.

"Packed house. Art, wine, a little too much 'philanthropy,' if you ask me," he chuckled, lining up a shot.

Franc smiled politely, as if only mildly interested. "I've heard a bit about that. A lot of good charitable work is being done down here."

"Good enough," Wes replied, launching a solid drive. "But that scene's more about who's seen than what gets done, I think. A little goes a long way for me in that environment."

Franc tucked that detail away and noted the dismissiveness, the casual suggestion of performance over substance. A pattern he was beginning to recognize.

At the turn, they stopped at the clubhouse window for iced towels and cold drinks. Franc sipped a club soda, glancing up around the patio perched overhead. A few other golfers from earlier groups mingled, some chatting with staff or shaking hands like regulars. It was a network in motion. He just needed time.

Mike leaned back on the cart bench, watching Franc watch the crowd.

"You planning to come back?" he asked.

Franc nodded. "It's not my usual tempo. But this place… I get the sense it talks if you let it."

Mike smiled. "That's Florida golf for you. Leisure on the outside, quiet power plays in the shade. But thankfully, I represent most of these guys, so be nice."

Franc smiled thinly, watching Wes and Clark rejoin them.

"Then I'll keep showing up."

Back on the course, the pace resumed. The strokes didn't matter. Franc had started playing a different game.

As the final hole approached, his phone buzzed in his pocket. A message from Sofia.

"Dinner? 8pm. My place. I'll cook."

Franc stared at the text for a moment. Something was shifting.

He pocketed the phone, stepped up to the tee, and took his swing.

Later That Evening

Sofia's apartment was tucked away above a flower shop just off Mirror Lake Drive, the kind of building you'd miss if you weren't looking. Old stucco, a wrought-iron balcony, and the faint scent of warm stale air lingering in the stairwell.

Franc climbed the narrow steps, his thoughts a half-step behind him. He hadn't known what to expect when she invited him. But the last few days had been about leaning into instincts, not logic.

She greeted him barefoot, wearing an oversized linen blouse and hair pulled into a loose knot. The inside immediately smelled like garlic and rosemary, replacing the outside air smell on the way up.

"I hope you're hungry," she said, smiling lightly, though her eyes, more comfortable, still carrying the tension of someone looking over her shoulder.

Franc stepped inside, taking in the small but carefully kept space. Books, art prints, an old turntable spinning something soft and French in the corner.

There were two plates set on a vintage wood table near the window. The intimacy of it was disarming.

"I could eat," he replied, offering a bottle of wine he'd picked up from a shop near Beach Drive.

They sat as the sun fell away, the windows casting long shadows across the room. Sofia made pasta with crab, lemon, and a touch of soup. It was a precise mix, and surprisingly elegant.

"You cook like someone who's had to win people over," Franc said after a few bites.

She glanced at him, then away. "Maybe I have."

The meal wove through safer topics, St. Pete's art scene, travel, their favorite corners of France. But eventually, the silence between them grew heavy.

"I still don't know who's watching the marina," she admitted, resting her fork beside her plate. "But they're careful. Professional. I see the same cars, the same faces. Never close, but always there."

Franc leaned back, nursing the wine. "And Tomas Juric?"

She hesitated. "He came around once last week. Asked about Caldwell. I told him I didn't know anything, which isn't a lie... not completely."

Franc studied her. "Do you trust him?"

Sofia stood and walked to the window. "I don't trust anyone who wears a watch you could sell for rent money."

He almost smiled at that. "Smart." Then looking down at his own wrist to assess whether to take it personally.

She turned. "Be careful tomorrow. If they know Carly's coming... it may change things."

Franc nodded, standing to help clear the plates. "I'll be early. And careful."

They didn't linger. Franc left with the sense that Sofia had given what she could but was caught in currents she didn't fully understand. Still, something in her voice tonight felt more grounded. As if choosing to cook and invite him in was itself an act of reclaiming control.

Back at the Vinoy, the lobby was quiet, bathed in soft amber lighting and the hush of late-night arrivals. Franc stepped into the elevator with a brief nod to the bellman and rode up to his floor, loosening his collar as the doors closed.

In his room, he checked Carly's flight again. On time.

He left her a voicemail, voice low and warm.

"Just got in. Looking forward to seeing you tomorrow. I'll be at the airport with the car. Look for the guy who looks like he doesn't belong behind the wheel. Travel safe, Carly."

He hung up and set his phone down, then walked to the window.

The lights of North Straub Park twinkled below, and beyond that, the dark silhouette of the marina. Somewhere out there, the moves were being made.

But for now, he let himself be still, sipping a glass of wine before turning in. Tomorrow, the game will shift again.

Chapter Fourteen

Arrivals and Intentions

The Florida sun had already begun its slow climb, casting a golden hue across the terminals at Tampa International as Carly emerged from the tram, designer carry-on in hand and dark sunglasses hiding a night of restless thoughts.

Her phone buzzed as she stepped into the main terminal.

Franc: Blue zone. Just entered the loop.

She texted back a simple: *On my way*, then navigated through the crowd with her usual ease, though still nursing a quiet tension beneath it all.

Downstairs, Franc circled through the arrivals lane, eyes scanning for her amid the swirl of travelers and waiting families waiting curbside. He'd hoped to meet her at the gate, but with her flight arriving ahead of schedule and the tram system barring non-passengers for security reasons, the best he could do was wait in the designated pickup zone.

The blue zone was bustling with horns tapping, vacationers dragging suitcases while bleary-eyed business travelers stared at phones. But amidst the chaos, Franc spotted her.

Even after all they'd been through in Bordeaux, the half-truths, and the distance, seeing Carly again stirred something anchored and unspoken in him. She moved like someone who knew herself, with a kind of presence and respect that grounded him in the moment.

She slid into the passenger seat, pushing her sunglasses up with a faint smirk. "You weren't kidding about the guy-who-doesn't-belong-behind-the-wheel look."

Franc glanced down at the resort's loaner car. Not the sleek silver Mercedes he'd been promised but instead a beige Lincoln, new but with the personality of a bygone era. "Be grateful I didn't borrow a Vespa."

She laughed, "The beige works on you." Leaning back, "It's good to see you, Franc."

He shifted the car into drive and pulled away from the curb. "Welcome to St. Pete. I figured we'd drop your bags at the hotel, then grab coffee. Unless you're still running on French espresso and croissants?"

"Croissants, yes. Coffee, not even close."

As they merged onto I-275 entering the newly constructed southbound lanes of the Howard Franklin bridge. The view of the bay was breathtaking as Carly rolled down the window just slightly, letting in the warm coastal air. Palm trees blurred by, and the bay shimmered in the distance.

"Catch me up," she said, glancing over at him. "I want to hear everything. Sofia. Juric. Whatever rabbit hole we're in now."

Franc nodded, fingers white knuckled on the steering wheel. "It's all waiting. But first, enjoy the scenery. After that, we dive back in soon enough."

By mid-afternoon, Carly had checked into her suite at the Vinoy, taken a quick shower to wash off the travel fatigue, and changed into something light but sharp. White linen pants and a silk blouse in a soft sand tone. Franc met her downstairs, waiting near the lobby's arched entryway beneath the soft glow of Mediterranean lanterns.

They didn't speak much as they walked, the silence was comfortable, filled with mutual understanding. The earlier coffee and a walk along the waterfront had reconnected them, and now, it was time to move with purpose.

They headed towards Central Avenue, Franc updating her on what had unfolded since her flight was booked. The round of golf, late-night dinner meeting with Sofia, the dead ends around Juric, and the curious presence of certain names - silent partners, rumored benefactors that kept circling back to Sunlit Canvas.

At the edge of the Arts District, they paused at a crosswalk near a sculpture garden. Carly looked at Franc, shielding her eyes from the sun. "You think Caldwell's still using the gallery to move something?"

Franc's jaw tensed. "I think he's deeper into something than I guessed. And he's not alone in it."

They reached a shaded walk-up Mexican restaurant window and settled at a table just inside the open-air patio, ordered street tacos and cold drinks, and laid out the fragments of what they knew.

"So we have," Carly began, ticking points off on her fingers before continuing, "a former associate with a history in Bordeaux, a gallery with questionable shipments, A mysterious yacht at the marina, and a missing man who faked his own vanishing act… all orbiting a luxury nonprofit and real estate shell company?"

Franc nodded. "And a possible red herring about a missing Cézanne. Which, thanks to Pascal, we've crossed off."

Carly sipped her iced tea. "Maybe it was bait. A reason for Caldwell to go digging and for someone else to keep watching who followed."

Franc looked at her, the gears turning behind his eyes. "You think we're the ones being led?"

"I think," she said, "if we follow the money tied to Vinoy Investment Partners, we'll either find Caldwell or someone even more interesting."

Franc leaned back, hands folded. "Then we start there. Tomorrow. Early. For now, let's get back and rest. You've crossed an ocean. Tonight, we breathe."

Carly raised her glass. "To breathing. Before it all unravels again."

Chapter Fifteen

Beneath the Façade

The morning light was soft, with a breeze off the bay that teased the palms along Beach Drive. Franc and Carly met just after sunrise on the veranda, the same table where he'd spent so many mornings alone with his coffee and thoughts. Now, there was a second cup, a subtle but comforting difference.

"I slept four hours," Carly said with a half-smile, "but they were good hours."

Franc passed her a warm croissant from the basket on the table. "Welcome back to the world."

They had a plan. The first stop was a contact Franc had arranged at the city's zoning and development office, where they'd inquire, under pretense, about the various business and nonprofit ties of Vinoy Investment Partners. While the company held a polished public image, one philanthropic, culturally invested, and community-forward. Franc knew the shine was often just lacquer.

By 9:15 a.m., they were in a low-rise office building near Mirror Lake. The clerk behind the glass recognized Franc from a previous visit, and after a few pleasantries, retrieved the parcel of files he'd requested ahead of time.

Carly flipped open a ledger while Franc skimmed tax exemptions and corporate filings. Halfway through the stack, she tapped a page.

"Look at this. Vinoy Investment Partners bought a warehouse in the Warehouse Arts District six months ago under a different LLC."

Franc peered over her shoulder. "Lighthouse Logistics?"

"Doesn't match any of their public filings. But that's not the odd part. Look at the partner on this one: Tomas Juric."

Franc leaned back in his chair, tension settling in like weight across his shoulders. "We found him."

"Or he found them," Carly said. "Either way, that's our next stop."

Chapter Sixteen

Smiles and Shadows

Sofia had met Caldwell twice since slipping the manifest to Franc. Both times, she'd told herself it was just to keep up appearances and to keep suspicion off her. But this third time, she couldn't tell if she was bluffing him or herself.

They met at Lonni's, a popular sandwich spot for locals on Central, not far from the Sunlit Canvas gallery. Caldwell wore a pale linen suit, too light for anyone trying not to draw attention, and smiled like a man who already knew too much.

"You've been quiet," he said, sipping his soda water. "Not like you."

Sofia shrugged, feigning tiredness. "The gallery's been busy. Franc Merlot's been asking questions."

"Has he?" Caldwell tilted his head. "Still sniffing around, trying to solve mysteries, is he?"

She didn't answer. Silence had power too.

He studied her, then leaned in. "You know why people like Franc get themselves into trouble? They think everything has some hidden secrets and that everything's a clue. That every shadow hides a key. But some shadows... they're just shadows."

Sofia just looked down at her glass.

"I'm reminding you that not everyone leaves the table with what they came for," he said, softly. "That includes you."

The message was clear. Sofia left before taking a bite of her sandwich.

Later That Evening — Flûte & Dram, Beach Drive

Franc and Carly sat at a corner table, the live music outside soft and jazzy, the patio just lively enough to fade into the hum of the evening crowd. Their dinner had been quiet with French wine of course, seafood, and conversation that circled back to Bordeaux and forward to what lay ahead.

"She's in deeper than she thought," Franc said, meaning Sofia. "And Caldwell's still holding something over her."

Carly nodded, sipping her Chablis. "But we're closer. That warehouse tomorrow. Tomas Juric is the link we needed."

They let the conversation drift then, swapping theories for small stories, laughter filling the gaps that used to be quiet tension. For the first time in days, Franc allowed himself to exhale.

After dinner, Carly called it a night. "You're going to stay and smoke, aren't you?" she asked, amused.

Franc smirked. "Only to honor tradition."

He walked her to the corner, watched her disappear across the street toward the Vinoy, then returned to the humidor at Flûte & Dram. He selected a Davidoff, something smooth and quiet, like the evening. The first draw of the cigar matched the taste of the wine left on his lips. Around him, people laughed and moved in waves. On the sidewalk, life passed without knowing who watched or why.

He liked it that way. For now.

The cigar burned slowly, each pull deliberate, the taste rich with cedar and spice. Franc sat with his back mostly to the street, angled just enough to see reflections in the wide window next to him. The crowd on Beach Drive had thinned slightly, as many families had gone home, late diners taking their time, couples strolling with the ease of a Florida evening.

But one group stood out.

Three men sat at a nearby table under a dim streetlamp. Not unusual, not loud. They drank local beer, passed around a basket of sliders, and laughed now and then but something about them didn't ring true. Their eyes swept too often, their laughter felt rehearsed. And they hadn't touched their food much.

Franc caught the glint of an earpiece. Small, nearly hidden. The man wearing it scratched his ear mid-conversation as if on cue.

It could've been nothing. Tourists. Locals. Off-duty cops. But Franc's instinct said otherwise.

He turned slightly, keeping his movements unhurried. From this angle, he recognized one of them but wasn't sure where from. Could have been the shape of the man's nose, the square set of his jaw, it rang a bell. Not from the hotel. Not from the marina.

Aurora's Promise.

Yes. One of the men Sofia had warned him about. Not the one with the flashlight, but the other with the phone pressed to his ear.

Franc stubbed his cigar just short of the final third and reached for his phone. No messages from Carly yet. He typed a note instead, just a few observations, time-stamped and coded in his shorthand then saved it to his encrypted file folder.

He stood, paid the check, and took one last look at the trio. One of them clocked his exit, barely perceptible. A tilt of the head, a glance over the rim of a beer glass.

Franc nodded once in return. Not as a greeting, but a warning. Saying, *I see you too.*

He walked the long way back to the Vinoy, through the park trails and avoiding the main street, alert but calm. The air smelled of dampness and humidity, while the night still held its quiet charm. But the game was changing.

Something was moving under the surface again. And tomorrow, he will dig deeper.

The morning sun broke later than normal, as a slight cloud cover hindered the glow. Franc and Carly moved at an easy pace, paper coffee cups in hand, the breeze from the bay just strong enough to flutter the hem of Carly's linen dress.

She slowed near an art installation in front of the Museum of Fine Arts, tilting her head as she studied the metal sculpture. "This city… it surprises me," she said with a soft smile. "It's relaxed but layered. Like a place trying not to show how much it knows. Welcoming only those it wishes."

Franc chuckled. "Sounds familiar."

They cut through the park to Beach Drive, where walkers and joggers moved past in casual routines, and families walked dogs and pushed strollers under the oaks. Carly pointed back across the water to the marina. "That's where you met Sofia, isn't it?"

He nodded. "Aurora's Promise was docked just there. Caldwell used it as his meeting spot… at least once."

They stopped at a bench near a banyan tree offering a shade respite. Carly opened her small notebook and flipped through a few pages. "There's something about this setup. Gallery funding, wine shipments, mysterious benefactors. All too neat, too deliberate. If Caldwell was using the gallery for laundering or smuggling, there's got to be a leak somewhere."

Franc nodded toward Central Avenue. "Let's check the block near Sunlit Canvas. Grab lunch nearby, see if we can feel out the neighborhood."

They strolled westward, past indie boutiques and coffee shops, the sidewalk filled with dog walkers, artists, and construction workers. Carly took it all in, the blend of sunshine, slow charm, and subtle energy. Her eyes lingered on murals, on street performers, on the small details that gave the city character.

At a local deli, they sat outside under striped umbrellas, their sandwiches half-eaten as they observed the foot traffic near the gallery.

"I've always thought places speak," Carly said. "You just have to listen long enough. St. Petersburg doesn't whisper, it screams."

Franc smiled. "Is that a compliment?"

"It's curiosity," she replied, glancing toward the gallery down the block. "Let's walk past again. Maybe someone new is working the front. Or maybe someone sees us and gets nervous."

They cleared their plates, left a generous tip, which they had learned is the common practice in America, and meandered back toward Sunlit Canvas. Carly stepped ahead slightly, scanning the storefronts with calm confidence, her eyes catching every detail.

Inside the gallery's window, a new exhibit was being installed, with abstract oils, bold brushwork, unlabeled. A man inside nodded briefly at their presence but didn't come to the door.

Franc whispered, "They're not open, technically. But he eyed us closely."

"Good," Carly said softly. "Let's be sure they know we're back."

They lingered just long enough to send a message, then continued on, arm in arm, blending back into the rhythm of the city as two curious strangers in a city full of secrets.

The morning sun finally broke over the newly developed towering skyline, casting light on the palm-lined sidewalks of downtown St. Petersburg. Franc and Carly moved at an easy pace, the breeze from the bay just strong enough to give slight reprieve from the increasing temperatures.

They circled the block, Franc keeping to the outer edge of the sidewalk, Carly quiet beside him. Something about the gallery's latest display felt rushed. The man they saw inside hadn't been there before. A fill-in? A cleaner?

As they crossed back onto 1st Avenue South, Franc's phone buzzed - an encrypted message from Mike.

> *Need to talk. Avoid the gallery. Meet at the Pier. Bring Carly. 2 PM.*

Franc slipped the phone back into his pocket, face unreadable. "We have a change of plans," he said, glancing at Carly.

She raised a brow. "Trouble?"

"Possibly," he said. "Or the start of the real story."

They walked the six blocks back to the pier, wind off the bay picking up as sailboats cut across the horizon. Mike was already there, seated at a shaded table beside a coffee kiosk near the end. He wore a ball cap low over his forehead and mirrored sunglasses.

"No names," Mike said as they sat. "Too many ears lately."

He slid a manila envelope across the table. Carly opened it slowly. Inside: surveillance photos, wire transfer records, and a printed roster of shell companies tied together by a common thread - Veltros Corporation, registered in Luxembourg with phantom offices in Geneva, Dubai, and Singapore.

Franc leaned in. "This isn't stolen art."

Mike shook his head. "That's the bait. Sunlit Canvas is just one gallery in a global laundering route. They're using art shipments and antique exports to conceal far more than forged paintings. We're talking narcotics, arms, cryptocurrency mining rigs and more, all moved under the same registry codes as fine art."

Carly blinked. "And the people behind it?"

"That's where it gets fuzzy," Mike said. "A network of intermediaries is mostly clean on the surface. But there's one name that came up repeatedly: Tarek Volodin. Private collector. Alleged patron of the arts. Real estate in Monte Carlo. Yacht in Barcelona. He bankrolls acquisitions and funds exhibitions that never seem to come to fruition or maybe even ever exist."

Franc's voice was quiet. "Does Sofia know?"

Mike gave him a long look. "She might. Or she might be being used as a pawn. Either way, be careful. If Veltros knows you're circling this, they'll come for you."

Franc nodded slowly, mind already turning over new angles. Carly tucked the documents back into the envelope.

"The gallery was a distraction," she said aloud. "So we'd stop there."

Mike tapped the table twice. "Exactly."

They stood together, the air suddenly heavy with the weight of a much larger pursuit.

That evening, back at the Vinoy, Franc and Carly sat silently in the hotel lounge, each with a glass of wine, reviewing the names and links within Mike's files. The scope was enormous now with private jets, flagged shipments, forged customs declarations.

"This isn't just a case," Franc murmured. "It's a global machine."

Carly closed her notebook with a gentle snap. "Then let's jam it."

Chapter Seventeen

Tangled Web

The next morning arrived cloaked in a haze, the kind that draped St. Pete's Bay area like a gauzy veil. Franc absently stirred sugar into an espresso on the Vinoy veranda, thoughts already tangled in the slew of additional information Mike had provided the night before.

Carly joined him, fresh from a brisk walk down Beach Drive. She placed a pastry bag between them and poured herself coffee from the carafe on the table.

"I haven't stopped thinking about that list," she said. "Especially the third name, Veltros Holdings. Something about it is familiar."

Franc nodded. "It came up twice on the export manifests tied to Sunlit Canvas, but under different shell corporations. They're laundering more than just forgeries. This is industrial."

He pulled a folder from under his newspaper. "Mike found an old customs leak, the kind of digital breadcrumb most people miss. These aren't stolen paintings going out of Florida. They're being imported into Europe with altered documentation. Swapped in transit. Sometimes entire shipments change destinations mid-route."

Carly's brow furrowed. "Art becomes the cover. And under that cover…?"

"Whatever they want. Weapons, data devices, pharmaceuticals, even counterfeit currency plates."

Franc leaned forward. "Sunlit Canvas is a hub. But not the operation."

Later that afternoon, they visited a neighboring mid-tier gallery on Central Avenue, posing as collectors. The manager, a thin man with theatrical glasses, gave them a tour of the works which appeared to be mostly modern and heavy on local artists. Carly asked casual questions about international partnerships. The man's answers were too smooth, too rehearsed.

"Has Sunlit Canvas ever curated art exhibits here?" Franc asked.

A slight hesitation. "They've sent pieces. We've borrowed frames and climate containers from their warehouse before. Good partners."

Too polished.

As they stepped back out into the heat, Franc didn't speak for a long moment. Then: "They're exporting crates under the guise of conservation transport."

Carly nodded. "We need to find someone inside that warehouse."

After returning to the hotel, Franc received a call from Mike.

"They're moving something in three nights. Port of Tampa. Shipment's registered under Lumière Foundation, bound for Casablanca by way of Lisbon. You'll want eyes on it."

Franc hung up and looked at Carly. "We're past art. Now we follow the trade routes."

She cracked a grin. "Good. I was getting bored."

The port was a thrum of steel and concrete, alive with the quiet churn of commerce. Tractor-trailers moved in and out of gated terminals with practiced rhythm. Franc and Carly stood in the shadows just outside the eastern perimeter, parked on an incline overlooking one of the smaller private loading bays.

Mike had done more than provided a tip, he'd arranged for a contact on the inside. His name was Dev Patel, a late-thirties logistics supervisor with a loose moral compass and a grudge against one of the shipping companies involved.

Dev met them behind the warehouse fence under the hiss of a flickering security lamp. He didn't waste time.

"Containers marked as medical refrigeration units," he said, pulling a folded sheet of shipping details from inside his vest. "But that's a lie. I flagged the weight discrepancy, reporting it's almost 200 kilos over what it should be."

Franc took the paper, scanning the manifest. "Consignee is Lumière Foundation. That's the same shell company connected to Sunlit Canvas's last outbound Bordeaux crate."

Dev glanced over his shoulder. "They're loading it now in Bay 6. You've got maybe ten minutes before it's sealed and cleared."

Carly looked to Franc. "We need eyes inside."

"I'll get you on the loading floor," Dev said. "But you didn't hear it from me."

Inside Bay 6

They moved quickly, blending in with the sounds of forklifts and grumbling dock workers. Carly wore a reflective vest Dev had swiped, and Franc moved with quiet confidence past a line of shrink-wrapped pallets.

The container was isolated but easy to find, guarded by two idle men who didn't look like they worked for the port.

"Private security," Franc whispered. "Not standard here."

The men stepped away for a smoke, and Carly moved in with a camera phone, snapping the shipping label and serial number. Then she pressed her ear against the metal door.

"There's airflow," she said softly. "This isn't standard refrigeration. It's vented."

Franc reached down and ran a finger along the container's underside. His hand came back with a smear of oily residue, too dark, too heavy. He smelled it.

"Lubricant. Industrial. Could be for mechanical parts. Or weapons."

A loud clang echoed through the bay. A dropped dolly, or a potential warning? Franc and Carly backed away, blending into the shuffle of departing workers as the final locks were affixed.

They were outside within moments, hearts racing, adrenaline laced with suspicion.

Back at the hotel, just after 1:00 AM

Carly uploaded the images from her phone while Franc pulled up port records using Mike's login credentials.

"The Lumière Foundation has had shipments routed through five ports over the last three months," Franc said, his voice low. "Tampa. Marseille. Rotterdam. Casablanca. And Singapore. That's not an art route. That's international smuggling."

Carly tapped her keyboard. "And here's the kicker: Veltros Holdings owns the intermediary brokerage in Lisbon. It's all flowing back to the same network."

Franc leaned back. "Sunlit Canvas is the disguise. They're hiding something global behind art, charity, and high-society events."

Carly turned to him. "So, what's next?"

Franc sipped his drink. "We go where the next shipment lands."

Chapter Eighteen

Time Running Out

The morning light fell through the tall gallery windows, colder, indifferent. Sofia stood near the front vestibule of Sunlit Canvas, arms folded, her gaze lingering on the far wall where a small modernist piece had just been removed. It left behind a faint square of brighter paint, a silent reminder of what had once filled the space.

The gallery no longer felt like hers.

The foot traffic had slowed and so had her confidence in what she was representing. The elegance, the whispers of prestige, the international clientele. None of it outweighed the chill she'd felt ever since Franc started asking questions. Too many things didn't add up, and she was tired of defending what she was starting not to believe in herself.

Her phone buzzed on the counter. A text message from Franc.

Let's talk soon. I believe you.

That sentence, so brief, undid the careful knots of restraint she'd kept tied. She stared at the message for a long while, the gallery silent around her except for the slow tick of the antique wall clock. The truth was closing in.

She typed a reply.

Thank you. I need to leave town for a while. I'll explain soon. Be careful, the both of you.

That Evening — Sofia's Apartment

Her suitcase lay half-packed on the bed, folded cashmere and linen stacked beside worn denim and a heavier coat than Florida ever required. She moved quietly through the space, not with fear, but with purpose. There were things she wouldn't return for, like dresses left hanging, and books half-read. This wasn't an extended vacation; it was a quiet retreat. For now.

She left a note with the building's superintendent, forwarding mail to a cousin's address in Wisconsin. The Midwest wasn't glamorous, but it was safe. She'd stayed there before during family summers, long before she ever signed a deal for high-end exhibits and was swept into the orbit of questionable patrons.

At the door, she hesitated. The weight of her choices, of knowing and not speaking had tightened in her chest.

With a final glance back, Sofia shut the door behind her.

Later That Night — Franc's Hotel Room

Carly was likely asleep in her room, and Franc sat in his, with the light low, scrolling through emails and reports. A new message came through.

From: Sofia

Subject: Thank You

> *I'm heading north for a bit. I've felt uneasy for weeks, and your questions forced me to finally listen to my instincts.*

> *I don't know everything, but I know I'm not meant to stay here and pretend anymore.*

> *Wishing you and Carly strength and clarity.*

> *Stay safe.*
> *- S*

Franc stared at the message. This wasn't about guilt. This was a warning and a goodbye.

He closed the laptop gently and turned toward the window, where the quiet lights of downtown blurred in the pane.

Things were about to escalate. He could feel it.

Port of Tampa

Franc adjusted his sunglasses as he and Carly stepped out of the rental car onto the sunbaked concrete of the port's administrative lot. Towering cranes moved slowly in the distance, silhouetted against the metallic shimmer of the Gulf waters. The port buzzed with activity, with freight containers stacked like monoliths, forklifts zipping past, and the steady stream of commerce pulsing beneath it all.

But it wasn't the volume of operations that interested Franc, it was the silence tucked between transactions, the sealed records, the privately owned shipments flagged under obscure foreign registries.

Thanks to a quiet favor from one of Mike's contacts in customs, Franc had obtained limited access to a specific series of bills of lading from the past quarter.

Carly held the printouts in her hands, eyes scanning column after column of shipment data.

"Here look at this," she said, tapping a manifest. "Four identical shipments, all from the same port in Marseille. Labeled as textile samples but flagged in two internal reports for irregular weight discrepancies."

"And all picked up by third-party trucks operating under shell names," Franc added, flipping to a logistics manifest. "No return documentation, no end receivers with registered tax IDs in the U.S."

He looked up at the massive stack of containers to their left with each one potentially holding something vastly different from what the paperwork claimed.

"This has Veltros written all over it," he muttered.

Carly nodded, lips tightening. The name had surfaced in their notes multiple times now Veltros. A syndicate, cloaked in international shipping and art trade, laundering wealth and moving illicit goods disguised through cultural channels.

"Remember we're not chasing stolen paintings anymore," she said. "We're chasing a front network using the art world as camouflage."

Inside the Customs Office

They met with the liaison Mike had arranged, a port compliance officer named Bennett, sharp and discreet.

"You didn't get this from me," he said, sliding a slim USB drive across the table. "But the moment I saw the Marseille shipments cross paths with a flagged consignee from Dubrovnik, I knew something was off. That's Balkan shipping but routed through southern France. It's clever. Almost elegant."

Franc took the drive and pocketed it.

"Anything else we should know?" Carly asked.

Bennett leaned in slightly. "Yeah. Keep moving. Don't stop at one link in the chain. These guys don't operate at just one port. They've got hands in

Barcelona, Trieste, Tangier... Tampa's just a whisper on their web."

That Night — Reviewing the Data

Back in Franc's hotel suite, they plugged in the USB and scanned through the encrypted logs. At the center of the document trail was a shell corporation registered in Monaco, recently renamed to "Galerie Vérité." A second alias used in multiple maritime declarations. They cross-referenced it with Sofia's gallery purchase records.

A match.

"It's not just racketeering," Franc whispered. "It's laundering. Using fine art as the carrier while moving millions through sculpture acquisitions, false valuations, and routed shipments."

Carly leaned back in her chair, stunned. "This is so big. It's global alright... and dangerous."

Franc nodded. "And we just stepped in it."

Chapter Nineteen

The Sting

Franc leaned against the stone ledge of the Vinoy's breezeway, the Gulf air carrying the scent of salt and gardenia from the flowerbeds below. Carly stood beside him, scrolling through documents and annotated shipping manifests on her tablet. Every layer of the syndicate they peeled back revealed another alias, another smokescreen.

"We can't move alone anymore," Franc said quietly, his eyes locked on the calm surface of the bay. "It's time to bring Mike in."

Carly didn't hesitate. "We need someone who understands both the legal side and how not to trip an international wire in the process."

Later That Afternoon — Private Meeting with Mike

They met at a secluded lounge near North Straub Park, their table tucked into a quiet corner. Mike arrived in a loose blazer and jeans; his usual easy confidence layered with a trace of tension once he saw the stack of evidence spread across the table.

"You two haven't just stirred the pot," Mike said, eyes sharp. "You've crawled into the damn kitchen."

Franc grinned. "Thought we'd bring a friend along for the fire."

Carly passed him a dossier. "We've identified the most active shipment trail running through Tampa, four companies, all traced back to shell entities. The goods? Most listed as textile or ceramics. But some match the manifest structure used in high-value art transit."

Mike studied the sheets, then exhaled slowly. "We can't arrest ghosts. But we can box them in."

Mike tapped his fingers against the table as they worked out the strategy.

"We'll need to time it right and wait for a flagged shipment en route, something traceable, and build a net around it. Not a raid. We don't want to spook them."

Franc nodded. "A containment. We choke the access, not blow the cover. Let them think the delays are procedural."

Mike's contacts inside Homeland Security and Port Compliance would quietly introduce new customs checks, citing random inspections. He also placed a discreet flag on any shipping documents that bore the name "Galerie Vérité" or the Marseille-based export ID.

Meanwhile, Carly would continue cross-referencing suspicious valuations and acquisitions made through affiliated galleries in New York, Lisbon, and even a recent one in Buenos Aires to build a timeline that could eventually tie the movement of stolen or overvalued art to laundering streams.

Port of Tampa

The sting moved slowly, deliberately. Franc watched from a distance perched inside a black SUV parked near the shipping yard while agents dressed as port auditors delayed the offloading of a particular container. They weren't looking for stolen art that day. They were tracking response times, gathering names from the companies that called in to rush the paperwork, and flagging the lawyers who showed up two hours later with urgent letters demanding the shipment's release.

That alone gave them a whole new set of players.

Reconvene at the Hotel

Later that night, Franc scrolled through a text Carly forwarded him. It was an anonymous tip from someone claiming to have worked for one of the flagged shipping firms.

> *You're not chasing a gallery. You're chasing a ledger that floats between continents. They never move product without three layers of cover. If you're seeing it, it's because they want you to.*

Franc read it twice.

Then once more.

He looked up at Carly. "We're getting close. They know all our names now."

Chapter Twenty

Checks and Balances

The next afternoon, Franc stirred a packet of raw sugar into his espresso in the Vinoy's lobby café, his phone set tableside, quietly on speaker between him and Carly.

"You're certain this doesn't compromise the broader investigation?" Mike's voice crackled through the line.

"Positive," Franc said, glancing at Carly. "We're not going after the full syndicate, just one arm. One cargo route. If we cut it without noise, it won't tip off the bigger players."

Carly leaned forward. "This arm's sloppy. They think Tampa's still below radar. If we isolate one container with a quiet customs stop, we can trace the handoff, maybe even find someone they send to clean it up."

There was a pause, then Mike spoke with careful clarity.

"Okay. Here's what we do. I've got a guy embedded in Homeland Port Security, a quiet player, solid ethics. We'll flag the next Marseille container routed to the shell company. I'll have it diverted under random inspection, while you two observe from a distance. Any actors that show up in a panic, we tail. No hero moves, no alarms. We track… and we follow the trail up the ladder."

Three Days Later — South Side Port Terminal, Tampa

From the roof of a low industrial warehouse adjacent to Terminal 9, Franc adjusted the lens on a borrowed camera, his elbows steady against the rusted edge. Carly sat beside him, holding binoculars, watching the port's silent ballet unfold with hyper-focus.

Below, a marked container bearing the Marseille seal was set on the tarmac, separated from its siblings. It sat idle for too long, unnaturally unclaimed.

Then movement.

A dark SUV arrived, parking along the side road where no pickups were typically made. Two men stepped out, one in plain clothes, one in a port maintenance vest. Neither carried tools. One checked a clipboard, the other surveyed the area.

"They're not drivers," Carly said flatly. "They're cleaners."

Franc zoomed in. "And they're nervous."

Ten minutes later, Homeland personnel casually approached, unassuming and briefed. They intercepted the pair with a pretense of procedural inspection. IDs were requested. Tensions visible. One man fumbled to make a call. The other scanned the area.

"And there it is," Franc said, clicking off a series of photographs. "Caught in the weave."

Later That Night — Debrief with Mike

In a quiet backroom of a law firm in downtown Tampa, Franc and Carly met with Mike over a map cluttered with red thumbtacks and shipping routes.

"Your instincts were dead-on," Mike said, tapping a newly added pin. "They were here to scrub the load. Intercept anything Homeland might find. They weren't expecting internal audits, they were used to smooth customs clearance from paid-off contacts."

Carly pointed to the Marseille trail. "If we keep this quiet and contained, we can send false signals back up the line. Make them think it was a random audit. Keep them operating… while we collect."

Mike nodded, impressed. "You two might have just cracked a gateway. And if we use this momentum, we may be able to follow the money and reach Monaco."

Franc leaned back. "Let's move carefully. One gate down, but there's a castle ahead. No flags yet. Just footsteps."

Chapter Twenty-One

The Game Behind the Game

Monaco, Late Evening, Casino de Monte-Carlo
(Private Salon)

The soft clink of Baccarat chips was nearly drowned
out by the distant jazz wafting through velvet-draped
doors. But inside the private room, there were no
distractions. Three men sat in silence around a sleek

ebony table, lit only by the gold glow of a Tiffany-style lamp.

A fourth man entered, sharp-suited and unsmiling. He leaned in, whispering something brief to the man at the center, an older figure with silver temples and Mediterranean features. They called him Devereux, though that was not his name.

The room tense.

"Tampa?" Devereux said, voice even.

The messenger nodded. "Container was held. Homeland flagged it. Two men sent to sanitize it were detained."

"How clean were the names on the manifest?"

"Fabricated. But they've already poked holes in the shipping trail. They'll see it links back to Marseille. And our man in customs isn't returning calls."

The third man, younger and lean, lit a cigarette with perfect calm. "This was a low-risk corridor. Sloppy. I warned you. Florida's gotten too curious."

Devereux raised a hand, silencing him. He took a long breath, as though measuring every possible consequence.

"If they start going after this, we'll need to cut it. Quietly. No waves."

He glanced down at the cards on the table, uninterested. "Pull the Marseille shipments for now. And get me names. Who's moving about in St. Petersburg?"

St. Petersburg, Florida — Next Morning

Carly's eyes danced over a printed report from the Port Authority, her brow furrowed. Franc, seated across from her in a quiet café off Central Avenue, scrolled through a database of shell companies on his tablet.

"You see this?" Carly said, sliding the page across. "One of the addresses tied to the containers is listed under Ravencore Holdings. Based out of a law firm in Miami but they share board members with three entities in Marseille and, oddly, one listed in Zurich."

Franc tapped his screen. "Ravencore just bought a property two miles from the Port of Tampa. The warehouse lease was paid six months in advance. No name on the ground lease, just a holding pattern."

They exchanged a glance.

"They're burying the money," Franc said.

Carly nodded. "And I'd bet they're rotating shipments to make one look legitimate by hiding it among nine clean ones."

A quiet buzz on Franc's phone lit up a text from Mike:

> *You've stirred the right ghosts. Good. Just don't let them know you're the exorcist yet.*

Franc smiled faintly, then looked out the café window toward the bustling sidewalk.

"We need to stay ahead of the curve."

"Then we go further in," Carly said, folding the papers into her satchel.

"Start following the owners, not the shipments."

Chapter Twenty-Two

A Silence in Steel

The warehouse stood like a relic of old ambition with corrugated metal walls sun-bleached and rusted in places, but the chain-link gate was new. Too new. Franc parked the borrowed car along a side road just beyond the surveillance line, stepping out into the humid midday heat. The building was nondescript, industrial, faceless but there was a stillness about it, a hush that didn't match the neighboring clamor of semi-trucks and forklifts at nearby loading docks.

He adjusted the new golf hat he'd bought at the Vinoy pro shop the day before, blending in as just another contractor doing a site check. A clipboard under one arm and a bottle of water in hand helped sell the look. He walked with purpose, looping the perimeter slowly, letting his eyes catch everything: the camera placements, the reinforced entry points, the subtle but deliberate lack of any signage or branding.

On the eastern wall, he spotted the only sign of recent human presence, a shiny new padlock and a small metal plate next to the entrance, wired and clearly tied to a silent alarm system.

"Too cautious for bulk paper goods," he muttered to himself.

He reached into his jacket and pulled out his phone.

He opened a secure chat and messaged Mike:

> *Warehouse recon: 1082 Atwater Blvd. High security, minimal branding. Confirm if this lines up with flagged manifests.*

A moment later, three dots appeared, then:

That's the one. Don't go inside. Infrared shows at least two on-site.

Franc slipped the phone back in his pocket, mind racing. He noticed a trash bin near the loading dock and made his way toward it, casually lifting the lid with one hand. Inside: plastic wrap, used nitrile gloves, fragments of a broken crate stamped with Cyrillic lettering and a wine insignia that didn't match any French exporter he recognized. But it wasn't the origin that caught his attention, it was the stamp on the label beneath it: a faint watermark belonging to Vinoy Investment Partners.

"So, you're not just a name on a gala banner," Franc whispered.

"You're in the shipping chain."

He took a quick photo and lowered the lid, stepping away just as the side door creaked open. A man appeared, mid-30s, stocky, wearing workman's denim and mirrored sunglasses. He paused, scanning the lot. Franc didn't flinch; instead, he raised his water bottle and gave a lazy wave, playing the part of a city inspector or vendor lost on the wrong block.

The man didn't respond. He just stood there, watching.

Franc walked calmly back to the car, every step measured. He started the engine, checked his mirrors, and eased into the traffic flow. As he merged onto the highway, he finally let out a breath.

Back at the hotel, he'd email Carly the photos. The logo match would help trace whatever false export paperwork they'd used to justify the crate's entry. But more than that, he'd confirm one growing suspicion: the operation wasn't just about stolen art or money laundering.

It was about the movement of objects, identities, maybe even people.

And someone was paying a lot of money to keep those things moving through Tampa without questions.

Chapter Twenty-Three

The Quiet Hunt

The corner booth at the restaurant on 1st Avenue South offered a perfect mix of privacy and casual legitimacy. Franc sat with Mike, a black folder spread between them, obscured by a ceramic teapot and a half-eaten plate of bruschetta. The sun filtered in gently, casting angled light on a stack of notes Franc had taken after leaving the warehouse.

"There's a routine," Franc said, tapping the map he'd annotated. "The shipments cycle through biweekly. The crates are logged as fine imports of wine, rare books, even antique furniture. But the records vanish once they pass the local holding facility. They're being cleared under false names and redirected."

Mike leaned in, his brow low. "The problem is we can't just seize anything without triggering noise up the chain. If this is tied to Monaco and beyond, it's bigger than our local office. It's federal. Possibly international."

Franc nodded. "That's why we play it like a leak. You feed intel to your trusted Fed contact, anonymously. Say it's part of an internal probe. If we're lucky, it brings a response that looks coincidental. No connection to us."

Mike sighed, rubbing his face. "You're gambling here." Franc smiled faintly.

At that moment, Franc's phone buzzed with Carly's name. He opened the message and scanned it quickly, his expression sharpening.

Found the missing piece. Ravencore Holdings is laundering through a real estate front in Marseille - but two of the board members sit on a shell trust headquartered in Curaçao. One of them? Linked to Vinoy Investment Partners. I've mapped the trail. Sending everything now.

A second attachment followed, marked "Structure Overview – Ravencore / V.I.P." Franc handed the phone to Mike, who scrolled in silence. His eyes widened slightly at the complexity of the flowchart Carly had created.

"Holy hell," Mike muttered. "This is a spiderweb. But if we can prove these funds touch the U.S. through Vinoy's shell corp, the Feds will be all over it."

"And we just did," Franc said. "Or rather, Carly did. We'll package this quietly, push it through your contact. No local headlines. No red flags."

Mike gave a sharp nod. "I'll prepare a confidential drop. We'll say it's part of an internal probe into international finance violations. They'll bite."

Franc looked out the window as a cyclist zipped past, then back to the flowchart. At the center: Ravencore. Beneath it: Vinoy Investment Partners. Around the edges, the faint watermark of something far bigger; logistics chains, charter accounts, and private vaults across Europe and the Caribbean.

Mike looked up. "It's a black-market empire. And Tampa's one of its doors."

Franc reached for his tea, calm but alert. "Then we nail this door closed. Quietly. Precisely."

Chapter Twenty-Four

Trail of Deceit

Marseille, France

Carly stepped out of the narrow taxi onto Rue de la
République, the Mediterranean sun slicing between
sandstone buildings like a knife. Her heels clicked
softly along the sidewalk as she made her way
toward an unassuming office above a perfumery. A
place she had visited only once before, years ago,
when researching provenance scandals in Southern

France. The man she was meeting was a well-known player in the art world, known simply as Lucien.

The hallway smelled faintly of lavender and old paper. She knocked once.

Lucien opened the door without a word. He was older now, leaner, with a slight limp and eyes that looked through people, not at them. He didn't smile but gestured to the seat across from his desk.

"You've brought trouble again," he said as she sat.

"I've brought Ravencore," Carly replied. She placed a slim USB drive on the desk between them. "You told me once if I ever found real smoke, you'd help track the fire. This time, it's more than forgery or theft. It's a global racket."

Lucien exhaled, then plugged the drive into a battered laptop. As he scanned the data, his brow furrowed. "Vinoy Investments. Curaçao. Marseille. Monaco…" He stopped, eyes pausing on a name deeper in the structure. "You've found one of the cleanest laundering rings on the continent. Or at least, the tip of it."

Carly nodded. "And Franc found the other end in Florida."

Lucien's voice dropped. "Then you're not chasing art anymore, mademoiselle."

He agreed to pull discreet bank records from his own contacts in Geneva and Marseille; such names connected to Ravencore through charitable fronts and shell investments. Carly thanked him and left, her pulse tight but steady. The trip had been worth it. The net was tightening.

St. Petersburg, Florida

Franc and Mike worked out of a side room at an attorney friend's office. A clean, unconnected space away from the gallery and the hotel.

On the wall, a printout of Carly's Ravencore chart spread like a constellation. Franc marked off sections with red push pins: port clearance contacts, V.I.P. shell structures, cargo handlers with past infractions. One red dot was placed on the container ID that had surfaced in the Monaco backroom meeting.

That container is now under surveillance near the Port of Tampa.

"This is where we squeeze," Mike said, pointing at a freight yard set for a midnight transfer. "The moment they move it; we tip off customs anonymously. It disappears into federal custody and the trail doesn't come back to us."

"And in the meantime?" Franc asked.

"We keep showing up," Mike replied. "Golf. Drinks. Gallery openings. You and Carly live like tourists, and we stay hidden in the game."

Franc gave a dry chuckle. "Brilliant, we're playing chess with no visible board."

Mike smirked. "Yeah, but we've seen their queen."

Franc's phone buzzed again. Carly's update from Lucien, including a name: Vincente LaRoche, an international financier whose holdings looped back to Vinoy Investment Partners and at least three Ravencore shell subsidiaries.

"I think we just found a new thread," Franc muttered, showing Mike the message. "LaRoche's the hinge they never expected us to find."

Chapter Twenty-Five

The Fabric of Deception

Franc adjusted his grip and took a shot off the 8th tee at the Vinoy Golf Club, the afternoon sun softening in the cloud-splotched sky. The ball sliced slightly to the right but just remained playable. Mike, walking alongside him with easy confidence, raised a brow.

"You ever plan to take this game seriously?" he teased.

Franc smirked. "You ever plan to stop talking on the backswing?"

They shared a quiet chuckle and continued down the fairway, appearing as two vacationing businessmen escaping the day's stress. But the quiet exchanges between swings held far more weight.

"Port scanner logs confirmed. Container 10837 has no customs trace from Curaçao," Mike murmured. "It's routed through three different flags before docking here. It's their preferred cargo channel."

Franc nodded, scanning the course for familiar faces. "And the men we met at the mixer last night. Marcos and LeClair. You sure they're not just money guys?"

Mike sipped from his water bottle. "LeClair's clean. Marcos? Not so much. He had a shipping badge on his golf bag from Kotor, Montenegro. Doesn't mean he's dirty, but he's not local either."

Franc's phone buzzed again. A message from Carly:

"Confirmed. Ravencore is linked to LaRoche Maritime Holdings and two shell vineyards. One in Lirac, the other a front in Marseille. Will send a full report tonight."

He stared at the screen for a long moment, letting it settle in.

"You think she's safe over there?" Mike asked.

"She's sharp. But if they know she's digging..." Franc didn't finish the thought. Instead, he handed Mike the phone. "Read it. She's found our hinge point."

Provence, France

Carly stood at the edge of a modest vineyard near Marseille, the wind tugging her scarf as she studied the shuttered estate. A rusting sign read "Domaine L'Éclaircie," but the vines were untended. No workers. No recent deliveries.

She'd followed financial ledgers through bank codes and wire transfers, finally arriving at this shell of a vineyard. Inside, it was little more than storage space with empty crates, falsified shipping documents, and a locked backroom she'd managed to photograph through a crack in the door.

The shipping codes matched containers flagged by Franc and Mike.

Back in town, she found a quiet café, ordered a glass of Viognier, and opened her laptop. The PDF report she compiled laid it all out: Ravencore had used faux vineyard holdings to export items under the guise of rare wine shipments, shifting artifacts, art, and contraband. The Sunlit Canvas in Florida was one end of the laundering circuit, but it was far from the only gallery involved.

She pressed Send. The report now with Franc and Mike.

St. Petersburg — That Evening

Franc and Mike arrived at a charity gala at the Dali Museum, dressed sharply, sipping some California wine they were handed off a tray by a server, eyes always scanning. Marcos was there, as expected, chatting with someone from the Port of Tampa's board. Franc leaned into the conversation, picking up fragments from an earpiece; logistics, rerouted cargo, an upcoming art auction in Palm Beach that smelled like another cover.

As they circled the room, Mike whispered, "Your girl's right. Ravencore isn't just shipping art. They're moving things the museums never even know are missing."

Franc watched a man slip Marcos a white envelope.

He nodded slowly. "And tomorrow night we're about to disrupt it."

Chapter Twenty-Six

Beneath the Surface

The scent of sea salt and diesel drifted through the air as Franc and Mike stood on a rooftop overlooking the industrial edge of Tampa's port. Below, cranes moved with mechanical precision, containers stacking like giant puzzle pieces under the pale-orange wash of the setting sun.

Franc adjusted the zoom lens on the DSLR camera slung over his shoulder and snapped a series of photos, container numbers, timing, faces. Routine activity to most. Patterns, to them.

Mike scanned through the latest customs log. "Container 19431. It will dock tomorrow night. Manifests say fine European oils and wine shipments routed from Antwerp via Lisbon. But -"

"But it was never scanned in Lisbon," Franc finished, nodding. "Same pattern as the others."

They both knew this container was the one Ravencore couldn't afford to lose.

Mike closed the laptop. "I've got a guy inside. Works on a dock crew. He doesn't know who he's working for, but he knows the rhythm. He's going to flag us if anything gets rerouted last-minute."

Franc leaned against the concrete ledge. "What about the camera blind spots?"

"Three we can use. Two are part of normal port maintenance rotations, offline for 15 minutes at a time, scheduled by a guy named Cameron. We bribe him, we get thirty minutes."

Franc raised an eyebrow. "That'll cost us."

Mike smirked. "Everything worth doing does."

They descended the fire escape slowly, cautious not to draw attention to themselves. The streetlights flickered on as they passed beneath them, blending into the city's undercurrent of traffic and low conversation.

Later that Night — The Vinoy Lobby Bar

Over bourbons and a shared plate of seared scallops, Franc and Mike mapped out the sting.

"We can't involve the Feds directly yet," Mike said. "Too many leaks. We get one shot at this without tipping the network."

Franc nodded. "So, we watch. Document. We hit record the second that container's moved and track who takes possession. Then we follow the trail."

"And if it disappears before it's moved?"

"We're out of time." Franc finished his drink. "We tip Carly. Let her make noise in France. Create a distraction over there while we move here."

Mike raised his glass. "To dual fronts."

They clinked glasses, a quiet toast to a war neither had expected when they first stumbled into this mess.

Next Morning — Clearwater Warehouse

Mike's contact, a lean man in a grease-stained reflective vest named Eddie, stood just inside the shadows of the warehouse, holding a small slip of paper.

"Shipment was relabeled last night," he said. "Container 19431 is now 19431-X and is being marked for private transport, a customs skip."

Franc frowned. "Private? Where's it going?"

Eddie hesitated. "Address is marked SEVEN HARBORS, LLC. Bayview transfer point. Some rich guy's compound, I think."

Franc looked at Mike. "Have you ever heard of Seven Harbors?"

Mike pulled out his phone. "Yeah. It's a shell. Been used in three offshore fund moves over the past six months. It's a Ravencore holding."

Franc exhaled. "Then we just found our endgame."

Chapter Twenty-Seven

The Waiting Game

It was just after 9 p.m. when Franc pulled the dark sedan onto the shoulder just outside the Bayview transfer zone. The gate to Seven Harbors' holding compound sat two blocks ahead, tucked behind a row of strategically placed high-end marine logistics signage and white-washed fencing. It looked unremarkable to anyone passing by. That was the point.

Mike sat in the passenger seat, watching through binoculars. "Two cameras at the gate, both angled wide. Nothing covering the west side access road." He smirked. "Rookie stuff."

Franc cracked his window, letting in the cool evening air. "And yet they've smuggled more contraband through here than we'll ever be able to account for."

"Not for long," Mike replied.

Their dock contact, Eddie, had delivered once again providing a copy of the internal Seven Harbors weekly intake list. The rebranded container, 19431-X, was set to arrive around midnight via a nondescript semi-trailer. No company name, no license trace.

"We'll split," Franc said. "You take the southwest side. I'll go east. If they move anything tonight, we get photos, faces, time stamps. We don't interfere."

"Agreed." Mike reached for his earpiece. "Carly's gonna love this."

Franc offered a tight smile. "She already does. Her message this morning said she'd matched Seven Harbors to a holding company owned by Belmond Arnoux's investment trust."

Mike whistled. "That's serious money."

11:52 p.m. — The Compound Fence Line

Franc crouched in the grass behind a low concrete wall bordering the rear of the facility. The sound of tires crunching gravel signaled the truck's arrival. It rolled to a stop by the loading dock, its back end facing the fence just thirty feet from Franc's position.

Two men exited the cab both wearing dark polos with no logos. Another stepped from the shadows and handed off a clipboard. They spoke in clipped French. Franc captured everything by video, close-ups, timestamps.

Then, another man emerged.

Franc stiffened. He recognized him instantly: Tomas Juric.

The man Sofia had feared. The same one tied to Vinoy Investment Partners, who'd seemingly vanished, now overseeing the offload like a contractor making weekend rounds.

Franc whispered into his comms, "Mike. Juric's here. We're stringing everyone back into our web"

On the other end, Mike's voice was calm. "Copy that. Got plates. Sending to Carly."

Meanwhile — Carly in Antibes

Carly sat in her rented apartment, hair still damp from a late shower, surrounded by documents and three open laptops. The name Seven Harbors had broken open a new lead. Juric's name confirmed it.

She typed rapidly:

> *Juric is listed as a 'consultant' for a Ravencore-backed art logistics company in Milan. He's been laundering*

high-value assets through the Mediterranean route, but his U.S. role wasn't confirmed until now. You just gave us the missing piece.

She hit send and poured a glass of wine.

Back at Bayview — 12:37 a.m.

Franc and Mike regrouped at a safe distance, crouched behind a storage container near the water's edge.

"They loaded three smaller crates into a black Escalade," Franc reported. "Juric got in with the driver."

"They didn't head for the highway," Mike added. "They turned inland. Probably toward the private warehouse on 4th."

Franc exhaled, the weight of it all pressing down. "We have them."

"Yes sir," Mike said. "We call in the team tomorrow."

Franc nodded. "And we end this in our own backyard."

Chapter Twenty-Eight

Setting the Trap

Franc leaned over a spread of aerial photos and intake manifests scattered across Mike's kitchen table. The sun filtered in through plantation shutters, highlighting blueprints, surveillance notes, and a half-empty pot of weak drip coffee.

Mike pointed to the eastern side of the Seven Harbors compound. "If they're using the holding shed as a checkpoint for 'clean' cargo, this is where we'll intercept. Small team, unmarked vans. We don't storm it, we let the container clear customs, track it, and seize it in motion. We don't want anyone alerting Monaco."

Franc nodded. "Agreed. The real value isn't the contraband, it's the network. Juric, Caldwell, Ravencore... we've hit a home run here." An American saying he had picked up while here.

Mike raised an eyebrow. "Could you have ever imagined it spreading this far?"

"All the time," Franc said, as if it was commonplace in his line of work. "But we don't get to pause and admire the complexity. We break it."

Mike leaned back, arms folded. "Carly still digging?"

"She's heading to Avignon today," Franc said. "More ties to Ravencore. Seems the tactics they used for art transport were a charade in Milan and was then duplicated in Arles, too. Shell companies. Shifting cargo. She says the ports in Nice, Naples, and even Split show the same fingerprint."

Mike gave a low whistle. "They've run this fraud over and over without drawing any suspicion."

Franc nodded. "Until now."

Later That Afternoon — A Meeting in Tampa

At a secure federal field office near downtown Tampa, Franc and Mike met with a small, vetted team: a customs agent, a DHS coordinator, and a U.S. Marshal. No badges visible. No names offered beyond first names and initials.

Franc laid out the photos, timestamps, and satellite routes. "Juric arrived on site at 11:53 p.m. last night. Oversaw transfer. Three crates moved without manifest clearance. Destination was a Ravencore-controlled property on 4th. It's quiet but we believe it's the staging point."

The DHS agent, a man in his forties with a perpetual five o'clock shadow, leaned forward. "You want a controlled intercept?"

Franc nodded. "We follow their route tonight. Pull them over once the goods are confirmed in motion. We can't risk alerting their base."

The Marshal tapped a pen against the table. "You're looking for clean names, too?"

Mike answered. "We're looking to unravel the middle layer. We can't afford another 'Gregory Caldwell' slipping into the shadows."

There was a long pause. Then nods.

"Alright," the customs agent said. "We'll loop in a maritime investigator. But this doesn't go past us. You've got quiet support. Nothing official."

"Just the way we need it," Franc said.

Back in France

Carly walked the narrow-cobbled street from the train station in Avignon, holding her coat closed as wind swept in from the Rhône. She reached her hotel and sat down immediately to email Franc.

> *The Ravencore trail runs through a private estate near Avignon. A shipment of crates arrived six months ago labeled as vintage sculptures. The property is owned by*

a Luxembourg-based fund. All signs point to interior transfers linked to the same numbered shells you traced in Tampa.

Be cautious. I believe they've started watching me again.

She hesitated before sending.

And for what it's worth… I miss you. I hope it's over soon.

Send.

Midnight in St. Pete — The Operation Begins

Franc stood just outside the warehouse district on 4th, dressed in black, earpiece in. Mike stood to his left. A quiet nod between them.

Tonight, they'd follow the crate. See where it led.

And if they are lucky, take the first real bite out of the network.

Chapter Twenty-Nine

After Midnight

The black SUV coasted silently along 4th Street, trailing two unmarked vans that had left the Ravencore-linked warehouse ten minutes earlier. Franc sat in the passenger seat, eyes locked on the taillights ahead. Mike drove, calm but alert, knuckles tense around the steering wheel.

Over the radio, a clipped voice confirmed:

"Vehicles matched. No deviation from the known route. Awaiting signal."

Franc checked the time - 12:14 a.m. Right on schedule. The Tampa marshals were in place along the causeway. They'd intercept the vans just before they entered the Port of Tampa security zone, out of view of any port surveillance that could tip off insiders.

Mike gave a quick glance toward Franc. "No fireworks tonight. Just precision."

Franc nodded. "Clean and surgical. We break the chain."

The moment arrived.

"Green light. Intercept in motion."

Three blocks ahead, headlights flared. Two cruisers, blacked out until the last second, slid in behind and ahead of the target vans. Tires squealed. The convoy ground to a stop in a narrow choke point along the access road. Armed agents moved with speed as doors flung open, and drivers secured.

Franc and Mike pulled to the side, watching through tinted windows as crates were unloaded under tight inspection.

One of the marshals approached their vehicle, giving a short nod. "It's what you said it'd be. Tagged shipping frames. Mixed crates. Tracking devices embedded. We'll be peeling this onion for months."

Franc offered a small smile. "You'll find Ravencore if we follow the rot."

"Our sting had numerous teams tailing Ravencore, Caldwell and Juric. The operation included a simultaneous takedown for everyone involved. You won't have to worry about those two men for a long time. You two have gone above and beyond doing your part," the agent said. "We'll take it from here. We thank you and appreciate your help."

Franc and Mike responded, nodding in agreement.

As they drove away, silence filled the SUV. For the first time in weeks, Franc felt like the wheels had turned in the right direction.

Chapter Thirty

Loose Ends

The next afternoon, Carly's call came as Franc sat on the veranda of a quiet café tucked in the alley behind the Vinoy. The storm had broken. Clear skies hung over downtown St. Pete.

She sounded tired but assured.

"I'm in Marseille now," she said. "One of the Ravencore holding companies here was just exposed.

Shell corp folded the same day the Tampa vans were intercepted."

Franc sipped his coffee. "It's unraveling."

"I sent everything I've found to the task force. If they want to chase it across borders, they can. I think… I think it's no longer our burden."

Franc looked across the courtyard, where a pair of elderly women fed crumbs to pigeons. "You've done something most people only dream about, Carly. You stopped something old and entrenched. You made people look."

She was quiet for a beat.

"I want to come back," she said.

"I'll be waiting."

Epilogue

Two weeks later, Franc, Mike, and Carly sat at a quiet table on the patio of a small wine bar in St. Petersburg. The sun was setting, casting a magnificent assortment of colors in the sky over the bay. Music played softly in the background.

They didn't talk about port schedules, customs forms, or encrypted shipments. They talked about cities they still wanted to visit. Books they hadn't yet read. Meals they'd never forget.

Their work had shifted. What began as a whisper of a missing Cézanne became the key that unlocked a decades-old web of international racketeering.

They had forced light into a place that had long hidden in shadow.

And now others would carry the torch.

They had done their part.

And somewhere, in the quiet margin between justice and rest, they found peace.